CLANDESTINE

BLUE FEATHER BOOKS, LTD.

For Mom.

CLANDESTINE

A BLUE FEATHER BOOK

by
Cheyne Curry

NOTE: If you purchased this book without a cover, you should be aware that it is stolen property. It was reported as "unsold and destroyed" to the publisher, and neither the author nor the publisher has received any payment for this "stripped book."

This is a work of fiction. All characters, locales and events are either products of the author's imagination or are used fictitiously.

CLANDESTINE

Copyright © 2012 by Cheyne Curry

All rights reserved. No part of this book may be reproduced in any manner whatsoever without written permission from the publisher, save for brief quotations used in critical articles or reviews.

Cover design by Ann Phillips

A Blue Feather Book
Published by Blue Feather Books, Ltd.

www.bluefeatherbooks.com

ISBN: 978-1-935627-78-4

First edition: August, 2012

Printed in the United States of America and in the United Kingdom.

Acknowledgements

I would like to thank Emily Reed and Jane Vollbrecht for liking what I wrote enough to sign me to Blue Feather.

I would like to thank Day and Nann for their guidance and patience with me during the editing process.

Also:

Renae, for being my beta and my friend.

Roselle, for correcting my Spanish and Allison, for keeping me in flying pigs.

The Raven, for challenging me to push the limits of my writing.

And Brenda, for loving me though all my quirks.

Chapter 1

The loudest lies are the ones we tell to ourselves.
—Eric Hoffer

September, 2006

 Tia Ramone was on her sixth beer chaser; each one had followed a shot of scotch. This was her routine, one she had fallen into far too easily on a nightly basis.
 She liked to drink. She liked to blur the line between her past and her present. That way she would be too drunk to think about her future. If she had a future. Every day it became more evident that she was slowly but surely flushing her life down the toilet.
 She didn't care.
 Her life hadn't been an easy one, but that had never discouraged her. Obstacles only made her existence more interesting. Fortunately she enjoyed challenges, because she had endured many, each of which had shaped her and pushed her to become the person she was. The tougher the situation she overcame, the greater her sense of accomplishment. At least that's how it had been. Now her only challenge was charming the bartender into serving her more alcohol before she was shut off and sent home or until some pretty young thing provided a temporary refuge in an anonymous fuck.
 She felt disgraced, disgusted, disheartened, and out of control for the first time in her life. She was slowly killing herself without the quicker, more efficient action of pulling the trigger. Suicide by self-loathing.
 Her lover was gone; her job was gone; her life was gone. The only things that made her feel better were drinking herself into oblivion and waiting for the next cheap thrill to find her.

Anthony Holt Montgomery, Junior, had been keeping tabs on Tia for some time. He had been pointed in her direction by one of his employees, a man who couldn't stop abusing illicit steroids even as his indebtedness to Montgomery skyrocketed.

Montgomery had a job that needed to be done, a job for someone with no conscience, no respect or regard for life, including their own; someone who could be blackmailed if their scruples made a sudden appearance. His muscular minion was too cowardly to do the job himself, regardless of how much money was involved. But to save his own hide, Bruce supplied the name of a friend of a friend of a friend. That didn't let the computer-savvy Bruce off the hook; Montgomery had other uses for him. As an enticement, Montgomery pledged that if Bruce completed those tasks, his drug debt to Montgomery would be paid in full.

Montgomery hired a prostitute, one he had employed in the past, to cruise the lesbian bar Tia frequented. She was to entice Tia outside to his car, where Montgomery would present his proposition. He was positive he could convince her to do his dirty work if the price was right. And he'd make sure the price was right.

She said her name was Roxi, probably a fake, but Tia didn't even need to know that. The second the auburn-haired woman occupied the stool next to hers at the bar, Tia had been fairly certain of her intentions. There were times when all Tia required for foreplay was "meet me in the bathroom," but she wasn't in that kind of mood tonight. She'd had a good day, breaking even at the casino on the wharf. This woman could work a little for her attention.

"So… Roxi, I haven't seen you around here before. Just browsing, experimenting, or thinking of becoming a regular?"

The younger woman caught Tia's eye, winked, and said coyly, "Does it really matter?"

Tia arched an eyebrow and fingered the torn label on her beer bottle. "No. I guess it doesn't."

Roxi indicated the empty shot glass and placed her hand gently over Tia's, which rested idly on the bar. "Can I buy you another?"

"Sure."

"What's your pleasure?"

A sly, lascivious smile curled the corner of Tia's mouth as she frankly appraised Roxi. "I thought we'd get to that later."

Roxi appeared almost embarrassed at having left herself so wide open with the veiled invitation. She emitted a sigh and a laugh at the same time. "What's your favorite shot?"

"The next one." Tia looked directly at Roxi. "Do you really want to buy me another drink? Didn't you have something else in mind?"

Tia knew Roxi was studying her. "Yes," Roxi said. "I did have something else in mind. But I really would like to buy you a shot, or at least another beer."

"I don't know if old Jane here will let me have any more." Tia nodded in the direction of the bartender and smirked at Roxi. "Besides, that's just wasting time, isn't it?"

"Boy, you don't mince words, do you?"

"Nope. Life's too short."

"You don't even want to do the obligatory 'let's get to know each other a bit' thing first?" Roxi asked with a smile.

Tia sighed. She wasn't in the mood for dancing around; she just wanted a pleasant, random encounter with which to end her day. She glanced around the bar but saw no other intriguing prospects, at least none as enticing as the sure thing seated beside her.

"Okay, you get one question. Make it count."

"All right. Hmmm. Okay, I think I've got a good one: what do you want most in a woman?"

"My tongue. Your place or mine or somewhere neutral?"

Roxi laughed, drained her glass, and stood. "Let's go to my car and decide."

Tia finished what was left in her beer bottle, said goodnight to the bartender who just shook her head in response, and followed Roxi outside to an Expedition with tinted windows. Roxi held open the door to the backseat and slid in next to Tia.

She straddled Tia's lap, took Tia's face in her hands, and moved in for a kiss. As the woman pressed in for deeper contact, Tia's long fingers slid down her shoulders until the thumbs moved expertly over each nipple, which swelled to the touch.

Roxi moaned as Tia cupped her breasts, traced circles around the erect tips, and started an almost imperceptible gyration with her hips. Roxi broke the kiss, hungrily nipped an earlobe, and worked her way down Tia's throat to her shoulder. Tia lifted Roxi's shirt to reveal two perfect, perky, and obviously implanted breasts, and had just sealed her lips around one rosy nipple when the car door opened.

Drunk or not, Tia's survival instincts were ingrained, and she immediately shoved Roxi to the side and groped for the .22 Stinger in her jacket pocket. When she pulled the weapon, Roxi unexpectedly tackled her and knocked the gun out of her hand.

Their struggle pushed Tia into the intruder and sent his 9mm upward, causing it to smash against his chin and take a chunk out of his flesh. He wiped a small trickle of blood away, bit his lip, and thrust Tia back to the middle of the seat. The cold muzzle of a Glock 26 was pressed to Tia's temple, and she stopped all movement, knowing she was outgunned.

Without saying a word, the man with the Glock eased into the backseat and closed the door.

"Look, I don't know what game this is, but I'm not into threesomes, *especially* not with men—" Tia began to say.

"What in the hell were you going to do with this?" Roxi asked incredulously, holding up the item that had fallen from Tia's hand. She displayed what looked like a tube of toothpaste.

The man finally spoke. "Be careful with that. It's a single-shot survival weapon."

"A what?"

"A gun. And it's undoubtedly got a bullet in it. Let me see that." He held out a gloved hand, and Roxi gave him the tube. He inspected it and arched an eyebrow. "CIA issue? They let you keep this?"

Tia and Roxi both stared at him in surprise. Roxi scrutinized the woman who had almost become her lover. "CIA? What—Montgomery, what the fuck have I gotten myself into?"

Faster than the blink of an eye, Montgomery aimed the tube at Roxi and fired; the bullet hit her square in the heart. Too stunned to speak, Tia watched as Roxi slumped back against the window, life fading from eyes that were already staring at nothing.

"Oops." Montgomery showed no remorse. "It was loaded. Imagine that. Is it still registered to you?" He didn't wait for a response. "Pity. I can imagine what the police report will say: They left the bar together and were seen getting into the backseat of a stolen SUV. The bullet that killed the prostitute was fired from a weapon registered to former CIA Agent Tia Ramone, the last person to see her alive." He smiled at her. "Looks like you just found yourself a whole shitload of trouble."

Tia took one last glance at the woman with whom she had been about to get intimate. Roxi had known this Montgomery; it was all a set up. Fixing her gaze on the man holding her Stinger and his Glock in his gloved hands, she shrugged in resignation.

"What do you want?"

Chapter 2

Sometimes the safest way to start the day is to go back to bed.
—Anonymous

Mrs. Anthony Montgomery hated it when she tripped over nothing, an action that this time nearly caused her to step on her own foot. Doing such ungraceful things completely contradicted her embodying the refined, poised socialite she was raised as, but never really believed herself to be. It was impossible to keep the stain of embarrassment from her face. She immediately looked around to see whether anyone had noticed her clumsiness and saw a clerk staring at her with apparent sympathy. Jody Montgomery grinned and tossed off a remark about a persistent tile that never failed to trip her when she shopped at that store, but the clerk barely reacted. Jody smoothed out her blouse, squared her shoulders, lifted her chin, and strode through the upscale department store as though nothing had happened. The last time she had been less than elegant, there had been many more witnesses.

Sondra Wainwright, Jody's mother, had been guest of honor at a charity event, the Evangelical Tuition Fund, one of her pet projects. Jody didn't agree with the concept of granting an already privileged child — almost always male — a full scholarship to Wheaton College. She had nothing against Wheaton; she just was convinced that the money could be better invested elsewhere. Jody hadn't wanted to go to the function, but her father wasn't available to attend and he had asked her to represent him. Her mother was less than pleased with her as a replacement, and the last thing Jody wanted to do was make the situation any more uncomfortable by drawing unnecessary attention to herself. So it only figured that she, a waiter, and a full tray of hors d'oeuvres ended up together on the floor.

The waiter had immediately scrambled to his feet, ignoring the echoing, clanging noise of the metal tray bouncing on the marble floor. He reached down and offered his hand.

"I'm so sorry, ma'am. Are you okay?"

She accepted his assistance and stood up. She couldn't help but notice that everyone was staring at them. She didn't know who was more embarrassed—she, the waiter, or her mother. Jody ignored her mother and returned her attention to the young man, who handed her a linen napkin to wipe the food off the front of her dress. "Yes, I'm fine, thank you. I'm so sorry. I should have watched where I was going." She began to brush away the morsels that wouldn't stain the material. "Are you okay?"

"Y-yes, ma'am." His expression reflected relief and shock.

"Are you sure?" When he nodded, she gestured to the mess on the floor. "Well, let me at least help you clean this up."

"No, no, please, I'll do it." He looked past her and his expression turned to one of defeat.

She followed his gaze to an older gentleman who was glaring at the server. "Is that your boss?"

"Yes, ma'am." The waiter immediately stooped to clean up the spilled food.

Jody knelt down to help him. "Let me go talk to him. There's no reason for you to get into trouble because of my clumsiness."

The waiter froze. "You'd do that?"

"Sure. Why should I let him hand you your butt on one of these serving trays when you didn't do anything to deserve it?"

He managed a small smile. "Wow, Mrs. Montgomery, that's kind of awesome. What does a guy have to do to come work for you?"

She returned his smile. "What's your name?"

"Albie—well, Albert. Albert Motega."

"I don't think there are currently any openings on my personal staff, Albie, but the South Shore Animal Center is always looking for volunteers." She winked at him. "Just a suggestion."

Jody informed her mother she was going to the ladies room to spot clean the damage to her dress. Sondra's tone and expression indicated disdain as she said, "Must you always embarrass me?"

"It was an accident." Jody battled the overwhelming discomfort that was brought on not by her lack of grace, but by her mother's attitude toward her occasional inelegance.

"With you, it is always an accident." Her mother folded her arms and looked away, as though her daughter's mere proximity was agitating.

Jody was quietly defensive. "Good Lord, Mother, I have the right to make a fool of myself every once in a while."

"If it is, indeed, a right, dear, you abuse the privilege."

It was always about appearances—nothing more, nothing less—and Jody never quite seemed to measure up to her mother's standards, no matter how hard she tried.

Joanne Dyson Wainwright Montgomery—Jody to her friends and relatives—was a very wealthy woman. Her family, descendants of the Mayflower Dysons, were so rich that the "old" money accumulated by her ancestors made the Rockefellers and the Hiltons look like paupers. An only child, Jody stood to inherit the bulk of the enormous family estate when her parents passed away, which would only add to the excessive trust fund she had already inherited. Because she didn't have to work, she donated her time, and an impressive portion of her monthly allowance, to hospitals and, her special weakness, animal shelters. It was fortuitous that she lived in a mansion. Since she had started to volunteer at the neighborhood pound, not a single dog, cat, ferret, or guinea pig had been euthanized.

The only shelter resident she hadn't rescued was a boa constrictor they named Beelzebub. The old boy had been found coiled around the branch of an apple tree in the botanical gardens of a local park, an irony not lost on anyone. No one came to claim him. If it hadn't involved feeding the snake other living, or once living, creatures, Jody might have adopted him, also. He really was kind of a sweet-natured guy. Instead she found him a home with a young couple whose beloved Burmese Python had recently passed away. They instantly doted on him, which relieved Jody since she couldn't take him.

Bruce Wechsler, Anthony Montgomery's indentured employee, sat at his computer and pondered the situation in which he was now irreversibly entangled. He entered the names "Anthony and Joanne Montgomery" into his search engine. In 0.23 seconds, the computer came back with approximately 160,000 matches. He clicked on "images" and studied photographs of the couple, sighing as he enhanced a particularly lovely picture of Tony's wife. Anyone who didn't know that Jody Montgomery was one of the Plymouth Rock Dysons would never have suspected she was anything more than a sharp, kind, beautiful woman, maybe a former college cheerleader. She had an air about her, one that shouted spirit and tenacity before she even spoke. People he had interacted with who knew Jody liked her... except, possibly, her mother and her husband.

It wasn't that Tony didn't like his wife, per se; he had married her, after all. But as Tony had told Bruce the day they spoke of the kidnapping plot, that wasn't because she was a knockout, or smart and fit and delightful, or sweet and lovely beyond compare, or even that he loved her. He had married her because she was worth a freaking fortune.

"If I had to have a trophy wife, why not her?" Tony had pointed to the wedding photo on his desk. It was after hours and Bruce and his boss were the only two left in the office. "She's not a bad fuck, either. A little inhibited for my tastes, but I can always get what she lacks somewhere else."

The confidence made Bruce uncomfortable. His personal assessment of Mrs. Montgomery was all positive, and even though all but one of his encounters with her had been from afar, he admittedly had a tiny crush on her. He had a sense that she was one of those women who had no idea just how gorgeous she was. His secret infatuation with Tony's wife, together with possibly a few too many shots of scotch, emboldened him to speak up. "Typical stud. Did it ever occur to you that maybe you're too selfish in bed to meet her needs? Or that maybe she doesn't actually love you and can't muster up the passion that should be found in a marriage?"

"Why, Bruce, you do have balls. I'm impressed. I thought the steroids might have shriveled them to the point that they had become ovaries." Tony laughed as he poured Bruce another shot. "It's not me, it's her. She's too... let's say, proper. I certainly don't get any complaints elsewhere."

"That's because you pay the others. Of course they're going to tell you how studly you are." Bruce downed his shot and set the glass down. "I guess... I just don't get it."

"Get what?"

"The real question here: why did *she* marry *you*? I'm sure she had her pick of every eligible bachelor around, and even a few of the not-so-eligible ones, and yet she ends up with you."

"What's the matter with me?"

"Nothing—other than neither of you loves the other."

Montgomery scrutinized him. "You want to fuck my wife." It wasn't a question.

Bruce covered his discomfort with a grin. "Come on, man. Doesn't everybody?"

Montgomery sat back in his chair and gave Bruce a look that made him shiver. Had Tony not needed him, Bruce felt he might not have made it out of that office alive. Then Tony pursed his lips.

"True. I do have an extremely fuckable wife. Isn't that what every man strives for? That his property be coveted by all the other property owners?"

"Property? You consider her property?"

"Read your Bible, man. All women are property."

Bruce blinked several times. "You read the Bible?"

Montgomery laughed. "Not for a long while, but it's not like there's a new version out. Face it—women are still chattel, it's just that the stakes are more sophisticated."

"Which brings me back to—how did she end up with you?" Bruce knew that his boss was an asshole, but the depth of Tony's contemptibility seemed to know no bounds.

"Why not me? The ladies tell me that I'm darkly handsome, charismatic—"

"Modest," Bruce interjected.

"To a fault." Tony's smile was cocky. "I own my own company, have impeccable manners, at least in public, and I roamed around in the same social circles as my wife."

"So did a lot of other guys. Why didn't she wait until she fell in love with someone?"

"I think she wanted to. Her daddy had other ideas. After finishing her schooling, young Joanne continued to show no interest in settling down and having babies to carry on the family legacy, so her father arranged the marriage as a business deal. She and I actually went out on a few dates, and it was pretty comfortable for both of us. Her father liked the way we looked together, and Jody got swept up in the idea of romance because Daddy wanted it so much. And, along with marrying into one of the richest families on the planet, I wanted to fuck her so bad I could taste it. So I took the deal."

"But why did she go along with it?"

"Because being married to me kept her parents off her back, and we agreed beforehand that if she found someone she actually fell in love with, we would dissolve the marriage. It was all pretty amicable."

"Does she know you've always fucked around on her?"

"Yes. But I'm discreet, and I always wear protection. I wasn't about to bring anything home to her and run the risk of being banished from the bank account."

"You mean you two have sex?" Bruce found that idea the most shocking of all.

"What can I say? I'm just irresistible."

"But… I thought it was a contract marriage, in name only."

"It's complicated."

"Is there a prenup?"

"Oh hell, yeah. Her father insisted we sign a prenuptial agreement, so no matter what happened to the marriage, I would keep my mouth shut about him setting it up, and I definitely would not walk away empty-handed."

"Except you have no intention of walking away at all," Bruce said.

Chapter 3

Crime begins in the mind. One only has to think wrong before he acts wrong.
                —Anonymous

After Montgomery had outlined his plan and what he expected from Tia, the two of them left the SUV parked on the side street around the corner from the bar, the body of the dead prostitute still inside. Tia walked closely alongside Montgomery through two alleys. Had she been sober, she had no doubt she could have disarmed him and shot him with his own weapon. In fact, under different circumstances, he would have been the one with the .22 bullet in his chest instead of Roxi. The real reason Tia had been unable to react quickly and as she had been trained was that she had been as loaded as her gun.

Montgomery drove his rented Volvo wagon for approximately thirty minutes, all the while listening to a CD of *Carmen* at a tormentingly loud decibel level. It wasn't that Tia disliked Maria Callas, but when one's head was beginning to pound, the strains of *L'amour est un oiseau rebelle "Habañera"* set on replay was a torture that rivaled waterboarding. By the time they reached the small wharf where a dilapidated speedboat awaited them, had she been in an interrogation room, Tia would have confessed to just about anything.

The Wellcraft 218 Coastal had seen its day, Tia thought, as she studied the beat-up, once-white fiberglass fishing boat/cruiser as it cut through choppy waves. Montgomery threaded it through a small maze of deserted islands and carried them to an impressive yacht anchored about six miles offshore, nestled inconspicuously close to a cay. Whoever lived on the yacht wasn't exactly trying to conceal their whereabouts but definitely wanted their privacy respected.

Hide in plain sight. It was a concept as old as the day was long, and typically it worked better than the authorities liked to admit.

"You don't have a captain and crew?" Tia asked, once they were aboard.

"Only when my wife wants to take a little cruise, and it's just the captain and a deckhand. Even then, she always returns to this luscious little location."

"It's certainly isolated," Tia said, "but still findable. Aren't you afraid the yacht will get stolen?"

"She pays a security officer to live on board. He makes sure that only authorized people come near this yacht. Any surprises, a call gets made directly to the bay police and then the Coast Guard."

Tia looked around. "So, where is he?"

"Because of his exemplary service and dedication to his assignment, he has been rewarded with an all-expenses-paid vacation to Tibet to do something he had always wanted to do—climb Mount Everest."

"Who in their right mind has that as a dream?"

"Someone with ambition." Montgomery's pointed look stopped Tia's sneer. "It will keep our conscientious young man away from the yacht and out of communication until his climb is done and this situation has come to an end." He led her on a walk-through of the craft. "You had best get familiar with everything and how it works. Once you and the missus are here, you're going to be spending all of your time together until the business is concluded."

Tia, a born cynic who looked both ways before crossing a one-way street, didn't trust anyone anymore, not even her own mother. She certainly didn't believe a calculating, obviously greedy, and murderous stranger meant "business concluded" instead of "wife dead." He had nothing to lose by killing Tia when this deal was done, unless she could get something on him in the meantime, something with which to barter. Best case scenario: she would do her part, collect the ten million dollars he was paying her for a job well done, and disappear into obscurity—exactly where she had been when he found her.

"How do you know who I am? How the fuck did you find me?" Tia asked abruptly.

Montgomery grinned. "It wasn't that hard once I knew what to look for. I do my homework."

"You didn't answer my question."

"Come on, Ramone, it's not as though you've exactly been discreet in your self-destruction. Reckless and careless are more like it. You have no one to blame but yourself for being at rock bottom, and let's face it, your behavior tells me you don't really care." Montgomery led her back to the deck. "All you need is a large supply of scotch and beer, and you'll be content. You don't really need to be sober to babysit a rich, spoiled heiress who is afraid of her own shadow. My wife is an undeserving snob who knows how to make the most of her birthright."

"You still haven't told me how you know who I am."

"I know that at one time in your life, you were considered honorable. Why you would throw all that away for a piece of tail is beyond me," Montgomery said.

Tia seethed at his conveniently abridged version of the actual events. Who was he, and how much did he actually know?

He seemed oblivious to her simmering speculation about him. "This is where you'll be keeping her until I get the ransom. I hope it's doable for you." Montgomery smirked. They were standing on the deck of a fifty-six-foot Meridian 540 Pilothouse yacht christened *The Quintessence.*

Tia swallowed the urge to attack him; he was the one with the gun. She tried to concentrate on what he was telling her, tried to stay with the moment.

Although she was not a stranger to being around material wealth, she was impressed with what he called his wife's "little getaway tub." The exterior aspect was deceptive; the interior was larger than most places she had lived.

Tia scanned the sundeck and its imposing entertainment system. In the other direction, she noted the direct, easy passage from the bridge to the helmsman's deckhouse, which included a cockpit with stand-up access to the engine room. Montgomery was going to show her how to drive the "tiny vessel." She could probably have figured it out on her own, but they didn't have that kind of time.

She followed Montgomery back down the molded staircase, unabashedly wide-eyed as she strolled around the galley that included a dishwasher, a trash compactor, a double stainless-steel sink, a microwave, stove top, oven, and a full-size refrigerator.

Tia had never been overly impressed by affluence. She had dealt with wealthy people before, but their lifestyles weren't excessive. And none of them had a yacht. Montgomery had told her that this was the smallest of three yachts owned by the Wainwright family. The Montgomerys and the Wainwrights lived a lifestyle that was excessively opulent, and she had a problem with that. People in that category were usually never grateful for their good fortune. As her grandmother had been fond of saying: "It is not wealth, but the arrogance of wealth that offends the poor."

Tia absentmindedly ran her hands over the smooth Karadon custom solid-surface, dark umber countertops. She studied the rest of the decor, admiring the high-gloss, cherrywood interior. "How much does something like this cost?"

"About nine hundred thousand. Pocket change to my wife's family," Montgomery said dismissively, making his way over to the bar. He pulled out a crystal decanter of scotch, a ten-year-old Talisker, and held it up to his "guest."

He removed two glasses from the shelf. "I'm going to go out on a limb here and guess you want some of this." His smile sarcastic, taunting, he poured some of the brilliant gold liquid into a small tumbler.

She abhorred his smugness, and the lose-lose situation he had trapped her in. Tia shot him a look that should have struck him dead, "It's the least you can do. And you'd better have more where that came from."

He sneered. "Ice?"

"And bruise it? I think not." She watched as he added a couple of cubes to his glass. "Ice is for pussies."

Montgomery didn't appear to be insulted; in fact, her words broadened his smile. "Living your life as a drunk and finding courage in a shot glass is for pussies. I'm giving you a chance to redeem yourself, show you can actually still do a job." He held out the glass, which she snatched out of his grasp and emptied in two swallows.

This is good scotch, she admitted to herself as it burned down her throat, but then she wouldn't have expected the pretentious bastard to have anything less than the best. It was warming and strong, and left a smoky, malted aftertaste. She savored it, feeling comfort in its richness.

"Redeem myself?" She arched an eyebrow and looked into the bottom of her empty glass. She shoved the tumbler back toward him for a refill, which he readily provided. "Funny, redemption is something that shouldn't enter this conversation." She tilted her glass toward him, and then at herself. "On either side." She raised the drink to her lips and threw her head back. The scotch disappeared quickly. It was even better the second time. "This is good stuff."

"We import it from Loch Harport in Scotland. They make it in the village of Carbost—"

"Like that's supposed to mean something to me?" She glared at him, bitterness almost seeping out of her pores. Her voice was harsh, essentially a growl. "All I said was, it's good. Save that pompous crap for someone who gives a shit. Your wife drink this stuff?"

"No." He didn't seem to be at all bothered by her rancor. "She sticks to her wine and champagne. The scotch is for when she throws little soirees out here, when her closest sorority sisters come to visit. You know, she needs to play the part: smoked salmon, oysters on the half-shell, grilled mackerel... and this brand of scotch. Ostentatious bitch."

"Riiight. Sounds to me like the pot calling the kettle black."

Chapter 4

The loneliest place in the world is the human heart when love is absent.
　—E.C. McKenzie

　　Settling into bed, Jody absently wondered when Tony was going to be home. She had gotten used to seeing him less and less, and she had begun to like it.
　　Most couples in their situation would have long ago opted for separate bedrooms, separate private lives. As long as they kept up the charade for public consumption, they could have easily perpetuated the façade of being the ideal couple without much personal interaction. Although they did each pursue their singular interests, Jody had very much wanted to be as much of a wife as she could be to the man she married. Even though their circumstances were a little eccentric, she had originally hoped that something more intimate would develop between them if they continued to share the same bed. After three years together, she had still not learned to love Tony like her father had told her she would. Even though she *liked* him and he had been a good escort for her at all the right times, the marriage hadn't become what she had hoped. Now she was no longer sure what she was hoping for.
　　They had yet to produce an heir, and her parents were pressuring them. Her mother had told her that if she was as clumsy in the boudoir as she was everywhere else, her lack of children was perfectly understandable. She wasn't about to dignify that with a response, or share the details of her sex life with her mother, but she felt she could more than hold her own in bed.
　　Sondra Wainwright's insulting sniping to the contrary, the reason that the Montgomerys hadn't had a baby was because Tony hadn't wanted one, though Jody didn't disagree. She didn't feel ready to become a mother, didn't really want to create children with

this man who was her husband. She couldn't explain it, certainly wouldn't attempt to expound on it with her parents, but her gut told her that starting a family with Tony would be a mistake.

They had been drifting apart. Tony spent more and more time at the office, tending to his business and, she was quite sure, whatever "flavor of the month" happened to tickle his current fancy. She was indifferent to it all. When they did have sex, there was never a question as to whether or not he would wear a condom. They both understood that he would, for protection against the pregnancy neither of them wanted.

Jody had even contemplated taking a lover of her own, but she really wasn't interested. She could barely work up the enthusiasm to have sex with her husband when the opportunity presented. The only reason she had sex with him had more to do with her feeling horny than it did with any feelings of love or obligation. Tony seemed to know just when she was "in the mood," and those were the nights he always made it a point to be around. Even then, how her husband "serviced" her was ineffectual, and she would shut herself in the bathroom and finish the job herself.

She had come to the gradual realization that her attraction had started to run more to the feminine gender. She had convinced herself that making love with a woman would not leave her unsatisfied like having sex with a man always did. Or would it? Was it her? Was her mother right in claiming that her lack of pleasure in the bedroom was the result of her own awkwardness or sexual inadequacy?

Lately her husband had begun to act even more strangely than usual, and Jody wondered whether he had somehow read her mind, whether he somehow knew that her curiosity about this new interest had started to become an obsession. She had never been with a woman, and the thought frightened and electrified her at the same time. As discreet as she would try to keep any lesbian experimentation, if she ever had the mettle to explore it, Jody knew her life was too public to ever keep such a secret for long. Her parents would probably not disown her, but they would never forgive her for bringing scandal to the family name, especially her mother, who would just add that to her long list of disappointments. Also, as much as the idea of his wife with another woman might turn Tony on, it would be an assault on his ego, and his behavior would no doubt become unpredictable and surly. She was all too aware that he had a temper, and although he had never unleashed it on her, she was not naïve enough to believe he never would. It was not just her reputation she would be fooling around with; it would be his, as well.

She laughed to herself. Here she was, looking for greener pastures when she couldn't even tend to the yard she already had.

Jody glanced at the clock again. It read 1:17. She sighed and turned out the lamp on the nightstand. Had Tony been right there beside her, she would still feel lonely.

Tia was getting acquainted with her temporary digs. Montgomery had left her there alone to gain a working knowledge of the pleasure craft. Accordingly, she poured herself another scotch and chased it down with another cold beer. She walked around the spectacular little boat, absorbing all of the comforts it had to offer. She wondered whether she could get the pot sweetened by having this baby thrown in. She could definitely get used to living here.

The full-width salon had numerous windows, but they were all tinted; that was good. She loved dark places, loved being able to look out when no one could look in. At one time, she would have chalked that up to job security, but now it was a matter of self-preservation. As she enjoyed the wheat-colored Berber carpeting against her bare feet, Tia ran her hand over the back of one of the two ultra-leather sofas. The port side couch was equipped with two recliners, while the starboard divan had what appeared to be a large drawer beneath it. Tia visualized herself relaxing onto one of the sofas. With a sigh, she snapped herself out of the daydream and continued her exploration.

There were three staterooms. The forward bedroom featured an island double-berth, a stall shower, and a private head. The port side stateroom had a queen berth, private head, stall shower and tub, and stacked washer and dryer. The master stateroom, down three steps and aft, was equipped with a king-sized berth, vanity table, salon seating, and a storage locker on either side of the bed. It also had a head, a stall shower, and a separate Jacuzzi tub. According to Montgomery, this was where his wife would be kept most of the time. Tia considered that a reassignment of quarters might be in order.

Regardless of future arrangements, tonight she would definitely take advantage of the hot tub and the forty-two-inch flat-screen television and entertainment system equipped with surround sound. She couldn't remember the last time she had watched the news or a movie or listened to music when she wasn't in a bar.

She strolled back up through the galley to the Bimini-topped bridge, where she admired the power sunroof, the entertainment system with its six exterior speakers, and the wet bar. She looked into the small refrigerator and found it stocked with two magnums and two dozen splits of champagne, and several twenty-two-ounce cans of Sapporo. Despite how she was about to spend the next few days, Tia felt as though a piece of her had died and gone to heaven. She hauled out one of the silver oil cans of the Japanese beer and smiled fondly at the hiss that followed her snapping the tab backward. There were some sounds she would never get tired of hearing. That was one of them.

She sat down on one of the durable distressed vinyl seats and kicked her feet up to rest on a cushioned bench. She gazed up at the clear sky freckled with stars, constellations, and planets, and dominated by the three-quarter moon. This is the life, she thought, an existence she could get used to very quickly, a life she might have had—for a little while—if her final assignment had worked out differently. She might even have left The Agency for that "piece of tail" as Montgomery had crudely called her, might have given up her job for the intriguing woman of proud Hispanic ancestry. Thanks to a co-worker, it was no longer a secret that Tia might care enough to trade her life for her lover's, and that leaking of information had been her downfall.

Well, isn't that just a bitch! Here I am feeling pretty damned good about having a night to myself on a million dollar yacht with all its amenities, and I have to go and depress myself by rehashing everything again. Who am I kidding? I don't deserve this kind of high life. I deserve exactly what I have, nothing.

I fucked up, and this Montgomery guy will probably find a way to kill me after all this is over. And so what? Maybe he would actually be doing me a favor.

Tia suddenly realized that she wasn't afraid to die; she was afraid to live.

Chapter 5

We look forward to the time when the power of love will replace the love of power.
        —William Gladstone

    It was after three a.m. when Anthony Montgomery slipped into bed beside his wife. She automatically turned into him, rested her head on his shoulder and slid her arm across his chest. As his cheek touched the top of her head, he envisioned his beautiful spouse, naked on their wedding night, not exactly naïve but vulnerable in her inexperience. They had debated whether to engage in the customary wedding night ritual. Neither had viewed their union as traditional matrimony, nor did they feel as a husband and wife should toward one another. They had both been caught up in the romance of the moment, and her inhibitions had been low as a result of the many champagne toasts during the reception. She was eager to please, and he would have been an idiot not to take advantage of that. Even though the sex got better thereafter, she was never more attractive to him than she had been that night. He'd thought then that their modern-day arranged marriage might not be such a bad deal after all.

    Maybe it would even have worked out if he hadn't gotten pissed off at Daddy Wainwright. Montgomery had his own business, MediMont, a distribution company that supplied hospitals, physicians' offices, and pharmacies with medicines, narcotics, and medical supplies. It was independent of the Wainwright fortune.

    Then John Fletcher Wainwright, his father-in-law, acquired the majority share of his company's stock, and even though Montgomery was legally still the boss, he no longer had control over his own business or the final decisions affecting it. Slowly, almost deliberately it seemed, he began to lose command of his ship, his authority diminishing day by day under the domineering influence of the possessively shrewd Wainwright, who professed to be looking out for his daughter's best interests. What started out as Montgomery's pride and joy, his one true, unassisted accomplishment, was now almost completely out of his hands.

He still enjoyed taking advantage of his alliance with the family and spending the fortune he shared through a joint account with his wife. That was all to his benefit. Had it not boiled down to a power, control, and survival issue, Montgomery would have left well enough alone. To the outside world, MediMont was still very much his baby, and Wainwright was content to let the customers of MediMont continue to believe that. But Montgomery hated to have to get permission to make decisions that steered the successful business he had started from the ground up. When his father-in-law recently suggested that Montgomery change the name of the company to MediMont-Wainwright, Montgomery was consumed by such a black rage, every breath he drew was homicidal.

If his father-in-law ever focused his personal accountants and advisors on an audit of the company to turn it into a corporation, they would be sure to find out about his other business—importing and distributing illicit anabolic steroids. Montgomery had a niche online clientele, selling the controlled substances to gym owners and managers, competition athletes, and coaches. His illegal inventory included Oxymetholone, Nandrolone, Methenolone, Stanozolol and Methandrostenolone, as well as a variety of preparations not intended for human use.

Long before he got hooked up with the Wainwrights, Montgomery got into the cartel, quite by accident. He had gone out on a limb, using bluster, ingenuity, and wiles to obtain Anadrol for an old college buddy. His fraternity brother's doctor had taken him off the compound because of the effect it was having on his liver, and because of the unpredictable and uncontrollable violent mood swings it caused. By then the steroid had endowed his friend with a bodybuilder's muscles and definition, and he was obsessed with procuring the synthetic testosterone by any means possible.

When Montgomery realized how much money people like his friend would pay for specific steroids, he was seduced into the enterprise by the old-fashioned deadly sin of Greed. From that illicit beginning, MediMont was born, a legitimate company he could use as a cover. The income from the steroid business was something that was all his, something the Wainwrights could not take away from him. If, for some reason, his marriage dissolved, the money he had stashed away, in addition to the profits from MediMont and the funds specified in the prenup, would enable him to live the lifestyle to which he had grown accustomed.

Now there was a distinct possibility that he could lose it all—MediMont, the black market import business, *and* the wealth he would gain in the event that his marriage dissolved in divorce. He was guilty of violating the only punitive clause in the agreement: breaking the law. He was desperate. That desperation had forced him to come up with the plan he had set in motion.

Even on his best day, Anthony Montgomery was not a man to be trifled with. His Jekyll and Hyde nature was legendary among his underground adversaries. Anyone who messed with Tony's status or income was taking his life in his hands. Literally. Tony was described by some as vicious and cold-blooded, not opposed to murder if someone got in his way. This was a side of himself he kept from his life with the Wainwrights. Until now.

It was unfortunate that Jody was going to be a casualty of the war between him and her father. Wainwright was hitting Tony where it hurt, and Montgomery knew the only way to exact his revenge was to hit the billionaire back the same way. It might have been different if he had been in love with his wife, but he wasn't. Though he was fond of her, she was an expendable pawn. With Jody gone, Wainwright's grief would be so all-encompassing, Montgomery was sure he could write his own ticket to the family fortune. There was serious money to be made. In fact, he was surprised that one of his rivals hadn't thought of kidnapping his wife long before now.

Yes, it was a shame his lovely little wife was going to have to go. He thought of her, terrified, in the hands of that burnt-out drunk, Tia Ramone, and he wondered if the former CIA operative's proclivities toward women and her lack of a conscience would prompt her, at some point, to sexually overpower Jody. He suddenly found himself aroused. Knowing this would be the last time they would ever be intimate, he stirred his wife with gentle but effective touching.

The hot water that had whirlpooled around her tired, worn-out body had relaxed Tia to a state she wouldn't have believed possible. She dried off, retreated to the large king-sized berth, and lay nude atop the comforter, flipping through television channels with the remote.

Tomorrow she would take the boat for a little spin and get used to how everything worked. Montgomery had told her that chances were she would not have to move to a different site, but in case something went terribly wrong with his plan, she should get familiar with how to pilot the vessel. Tomorrow evening she would pick up the package and deliver it to the yacht, and the assignment would begin. Montgomery had not said that he wanted his wife to be permanently eliminated, but Tia knew that the death of the heiress would be the finale most beneficial to her husband.

Tia had killed, in the line of duty. She had learned at spy school in Camp Perry, Virginia, also known as The Farm, how to disengage her mind from her body in order to kill with little psychological aftereffect. After all, the three individuals she had disposed of had either personally engaged in or ordered multiple crimes carried out against the United States, as defined in her CIA bible. Her targets had been ruthless, without conscience, would have thought nothing of spilling a child's blood to save their own skins, much less of sending Tia to meet her Maker. She wouldn't go so far as to say they deserved execution, but in her view, the world was better off without them.

On the other hand, this woman she was about to abduct and hold for ransom had done nothing other than be born into an obscenely wealthy family and, obviously, marry the wrong guy. Still, the lure of a ten-million-dollar payment might be enough to persuade Tia to go through with killing Montgomery's wife, if that's what he wanted in the end... and she was convinced it was. She was also certain that, should something go awry, Montgomery would not hesitate to point a finger in her direction to take any heat off of him.

She sighed and blinked sleep out of her eyes. She was getting way ahead of herself. She would analyze her options more clearly in the morning. Until then, the exquisite feel of the European baffle box, goose down comforter against her skin was luscious and quickly lulled her toward slumber. *People say that the best sedative is a clear conscience. Judging by me, I guess that's a myth.*

Chapter 6

A true test of someone's character is not what they do in the light but what they do in the dark.
—Anonymous

When Jody woke, Montgomery was gone. She blinked away the last fragments of sleep and stretched out her leg muscles, the memory of making love creeping into her mind. Her eyes snapped open as the visual of her husband's performance on top of her came into focus. Startled, she leaned up on her elbows, feeling the reminders of intercourse that lingered around her lower body. She thought she had dreamt it.

She was torn between anger and surprise as she tried to recall when Montgomery had arrived home, and when they had gotten affectionate. The prescription sleep aid she took to battle her insomnia made it all too misty for her, but she was pretty sure she had not initiated intimacy. It was unusual for him to behave so selfishly relative to their sex life, and as he had left some of himself on and inside her, it was clear he had not used a condom. Jody pounded her fist on the bed, rolled over to a sitting position, and reached for her cellular phone. She speed dialed his cell number, got his voice mail, and hung up. She glanced at her alarm clock. 10:27. She called his work number.

"Nina, this is Jody. Is my husband there?"

"Yes, Jody. He just got out of a meeting," his secretary said. "Hang on."

The longer she waited on hold, the more agitated Jody became. They had an agreement, for God's sake. The irritant was not that he might have gotten her pregnant, but that he might have given her some disease. She was pretty sure he was as careful about using protection with his other women as he was with her—Montgomery seemed to be one of the rare men who actually enjoyed wearing a condom—but she had only his word for that. He had never given her any reason to disbelieve him, but to do what he had done to her while she was semiconscious was unacceptable.

"Hi, Mrs. Montgomery." There was a smile and fondness in his voice she was not used to and it threw her off-guard, rendering her momentarily speechless. "Thank you for last night."

He was *thanking* her for sex? Who was this man, and what had he done with her husband? "Tony... what's going on?"

"What do you mean?"

Nonplussed, her reaction was to laugh. "What do I mean? Well, first, we had unprotected sex and, second, since when do you just climb on board without, well, not just my permission, but not even my knowledge?"

"You didn't seem to mind last night."

His tone was playful, teasing, and again it stymied her. Finally she said, "When was the last time you were tested for any kind of STD?"

"Last week, and I'm clean, and I haven't been with anyone else in over a month."

That could easily be a lie, but she let that point slide. "What if I'm pregnant?"

"If you're really concerned, call Dr. Santos and get a morning-after pill. But... would it really be so bad to produce an heir to get your parents off our backs?"

"Tony!" She was flustered to the point of stammering. "I... you..." She took a deep breath, closed her eyes, and concentrated. "We talked about this. You may have changed your mind about having children, but I haven't changed mine. And that also doesn't address the issue of your having sex with me without my consent."

"You make it sound like rape."

He didn't sound defensive or insulted, he sounded... smug. "In a way," she said quietly, "it was."

"Like I said, you didn't seem to mind last night. Look, let me make it up to you. I'll call Santos for you, and you can stop by his office in an hour, and then why don't you meet me at The Cypress for dinner?"

They hadn't had dinner at the most expensive restaurant in town since they had celebrated their third anniversary there. She had recently been there twice for charity events, but not with her husband. She tried not to be suspicious, but his manner was too solicitous. "Never mind calling Santos. Tony, what's going on?"

"Nothing. I'd just like to have a nice dinner out with my beautiful wife. I realize that we don't have a traditional marriage, but occasionally I like to feel like your husband in a more intimate way. Don't worry. It's a phase. It will pass," he added, his inexplicable good humor clear in his voice.

She considered his explanation. It sounded plausible enough. She sighed. "Just… wake me up next time, okay?" If there was a next time, she thought. She was still pretty steamed.

"Okay. I promise."

"What time do you want to meet at The Cypress?"

"Six works for me."

"Okay. I'll see you there." She hung up more confused than before she had called him. He sounded satisfied with himself, yet genial. He was up to something.

Tia took the modest yacht out for a ride around the collection of small, uninhabited islands amid which it had been nestled. It was a powerful craft and complicated to maneuver. Fortunately she was a quick study and had absorbed the instructions that Montgomery had written out for her. It also didn't hurt that almost all functions in the pilothouse seemed to be color-coded. After three hours of making wide circles and steering the yacht in and out of the cays like running an obstacle course, Tia felt confident that she could move *The Quintessence* in a hurry, if circumstances dictated.

Before embarking on her assignment, Tia relaxed and reviewed her instructions one last time. As long as Montgomery's wife was where Montgomery said she would be, it should be no problem to carry out the abduction phase of the mission. She wasn't as certain about where the rest of the project was going to take her. She wondered if Roxi's corpse had been discovered, and if so, whether the police had traced the fingerprints in the car, the saliva on the body, and, even more incriminating, the Stinger Montgomery left on the floor in the backseat. She had not yet heard anything on the news about a dead prostitute being found in a stolen car near Tia's former favorite watering hole, and even though scenarios like that weren't exactly commonplace, maybe the press didn't feel it was a big enough story to report. However, should word get around that the hooker was allegedly murdered by a disgraced female CIA operative in sordid circumstances, shit would definitely hit the fan.

Tia really wanted, needed a drink, but knew it was best to stay sober until she was back on the yacht with her package. For the first time since she'd left The Agency, she was not well on her way to being drunk by noon.

Chapter 7

Never judge a person's actions until you know their motives.
—Anonymous

The restaurant was crowded and noisy, just the way Montgomery had hoped it would be. The more witnesses there were to how cozy he and his wife looked together, the better it would be for him.

They shared a pleasant meal and some neutral conversation, both avoiding the touchy subject of the previous night.

Once Jody felt the effects of the drug Montgomery had smoothly put in her second glass of wine, it wouldn't be long before she felt groggy. She was a responsible woman and would pull over rather than drive while sleepy.

By practicing on Bruce, Montgomery had calculated the distance Jody would be able to put between herself and the restaurant before the sedative took full effect. He had accounted for the difference in weight, administering a slightly higher dosage to the steroid-abusing young man than he would to his one hundred-and-eight pound wife. Bruce had very specific instructions to drive the fixed route Jody always took from that area of town and pull over at the first sign of being overtaken by sleep. Each practice run, Bruce took refuge at the same rest stop, which was not highly populated and not extremely well lit, but appeared to be safe. This would be the perfect place for Tia to walk out of the shadows, get into Jody's car, move her to the passenger side, and drive away.

Montgomery shook with anticipation of the plan finally being put into motion, the fear of something going wrong, and just a twinge of sadness. Sex with Jody had been very hot the night before, even if she hadn't been awake enough to fully participate, and she looked particularly bewitching at dinner. When she walked into the restaurant to meet him, she had captured the eye of every red-blooded male in the place, and he took satisfaction from that, his ego being what it was. As much as he hated to admit it, he would miss her, but Wainwright was to blame. If Jody's father hadn't gotten so unreasonably covetous, retaliation wouldn't have been necessary.

Still, as they waited for the valet to bring up their cars, he couldn't stop thinking about how beautiful she had become over the short span of their marriage. She had matured, and, even though she was still Daddy's girl, she had no problem standing up to her pretentious parents when their convictions didn't match her own. She had also become quite adept at defending him when either her mother or father decided to take a verbal potshot at him. No, he and Jody were not in love, but he had grown to love her in his own way. He studied her intently one last time before she got in her car and drove away.

What a waste.

He left The Cypress for his weekly Pai Gow game at the club with a group of the town's more prestigious businessmen, a perfect alibi for his whereabouts at the time of her disappearance. Before he exited the restaurant parking lot, he contacted Tia via an untraceable disposable cell phone and made sure she was at the rendezvous point.

Tia tied off the motor-driven dinghy from *The Quintessence* at a deserted, unlit dock about two miles from the rest stop and jogged along the beach to the approximate location. She walked through the forested area and into the wooded rest stop, where she spotted the Mercedes GL450 and observed the still figure in the driver's seat. Tia looked around and confirmed that the occupants of the four other vehicles in the rest area weren't paying any attention to Jody Montgomery's SUV. They were tending to their business—using the restroom, buying refreshments from the vending machines, checking maps, and exercising pets and themselves. When the last of the cars had driven off, Tia walked swiftly to the gunmetal-gray vehicle. She unlocked the door with the duplicate key Montgomery had provided, moved Jody's unconscious form over the console to the passenger side, and drove back to the deserted dock.

She was able to ease the Mercedes close to the dock without having to drive off the pavement, thereby not leaving any deep tire tracks that might not be washed away in a timely manner by the tide. After transferring Jody to the dinghy, she covered her with a tarp. She removed the battery from Jody's cell phone, tossed it into the ocean, and kept the phone itself. The signal couldn't be traced if anyone tried to zone in on the pings before the battery died. She then drove the car a quarter-mile away and parked it in a storage unit rented in Bruce's name over a month before.

Tia detached the license plates, removed the other identifying information from the vehicle, and took it all with her to discard in the ocean. Montgomery had already removed the vehicle recovery system and replaced the VIN on the dashboard and driver's side door with a fraudulent number. It wouldn't throw the authorities off for long if they located the SUV, but Montgomery said it would buy some time if the vehicle was discovered, which he was quite sure it wouldn't be. To link his wife with Bruce Wechsler in any way would be a stretch; Bruce and Mrs. Montgomery supposedly never had any contact, and Montgomery was making sure that Bruce had arranged a solid alibi for the time frame in which Jody disappeared.

Tia shook her head in recognition of the fact that everyone involved had an alibi except her. Montgomery was definitely setting her up to take the fall. She closed and padlocked the roll-down door of the storage unit. She jogged back to the small motorboat that held the covered, unconscious form of Jody Montgomery and launched the boat onto the water.

Fireman-style, Tia carried Jody's limp body onto the yacht and deposited her on the berth in the master stateroom. She made sure Jody's respiration was as regular as it should be under the influence of the drug. Tia locked her inside and returned to the dinghy, which she secured to the bigger craft. The water had become choppy, and she wanted to ensure that the small boat was firmly tethered to *The Quintessence*. She climbed back aboard the yacht and went to check on her captive.

At the port side of the king-sized bed where she had slept so peacefully the night before, Tia looked into the face of Mrs. Anthony Montgomery, illuminated by light shining into the room from the door to the salon. Tia was startled by what she saw.

This woman appeared younger, slighter than in the photograph Montgomery had given her or those she had seen in scattered press releases. Jody's features—at least in her current state—seemed unmarked by the contempt, maliciousness, and deviousness that consumed her husband, traits he wore like armor. Tia was well aware that looks could be deceiving, but instinct told her this woman was not that way. Before she realized it, she had reached over and pushed a tendril of blonde hair away from the wan face.

Tia quickly drew her hand away. She made sure Jody at least looked comfortable, left the room, and secured the door.

It was done. The car was hidden, the vehicle identification disposed of, the dinghy tied up, and the prisoner safely in her custody. Now she would wait for instructions from Montgomery.

She was only to contact him if something had gone wrong; if not, he would call her on his way home, after his poker game. The plan had been carried out with nearly military precision, just as though she were back at The Agency, and she felt life surge through her again.

Tia moved to the bar and poured herself a double shot from the decanter of scotch. When that was gone, another demitasse full of the dark amber liquid disappeared down her throat.

She would crack open a cold beer after her shower.

Jody fluttered into a consciousness that was painful and disoriented. It took her a few minutes to recognize she wasn't in her car. She let her eyes adjust to the darkness and looked around for a lamp or light switch.

Thanks to the moonlight that filtered through the porthole, objects in the room began to come into focus. Then it hit her. The circular window meant she was probably on her yacht, without any earthly idea how she had gotten there. Her attempt to sit up was a mistake. A searing pain of migraine proportions sliced across her forehead, making her feel dizzy and nauseous. She lay down, closed her eyes, and felt her head for a lump or bruise but found nothing.

She slowly rolled to her side and reached for the bedside light, only to find it wasn't working. Again she tried to sit up, managing the throbbing ache that attacked her skull and the queasiness that clawed at her stomach. What the hell happened? How did she get onto *The Quintessence?* Why did her head hurt so badly? She shakily stood, reached out to steady herself against the vanity, got her bearings, and struggled to the door. The whirling and nausea began to subside, and the hammering in her head lessened by the second. She twisted the handle and was stunned to find the door locked from the outside. She felt above the doorknob where the flip lock should be, but it was gone. Her curiosity quickly turned to alarm when she tugged on the handle and the door wouldn't budge.

"Hello? Hey... hello! Kevin?" Capable of cogent thought again, her mind raced. What the hell was going on? "Kevin! Open the door! Let me out of here!" She pounded on the door and the wall, to no avail. She stopped, placed her ear to the door, and listened. She heard nothing on the other side, no sound of movement. Where was Kevin?

Jody paced the length of the stateroom. Although unsettled, she tried not to panic. The last thing she recalled was getting sleepy and pulling into the rest stop. Before that… Before that was dinner at The Cypress. She and Tony had a nice dinner, and she had two glasses of wine. Nothing out of the ordinary there. But getting so sleepy that she had to pull over, that was odd. Two glasses of wine did not get her drunk. Had someone slipped something into her wine? Not possible. She never left the table, and the only person who came near it was their server. Had some medical emergency caused her to pass out? If so, why wasn't she in a hospital? There was only one way to find any answers. Probing her belt for her cell phone, she was surprised to find it missing. Now she was feeling some major fear. *What the fuck is happening here?*

Tia shut off the water, stepped out of the shower stall, and wrapped a huge bath towel around her body. She pressed the excess water out of her hair and smiled at the thought of the hot tub working the soreness out of her bones. Except, if she indulged in the luxury tonight, she would have to use the deck Jacuzzi. She opened the door to the storage area in the stateroom, pulled out a T-shirt and a pair of thin, cotton lounging pants that must have belonged to Montgomery, and put them on. Although a little big, they covered her. That's all she cared about. She exited the stateroom to the salon, crossed to the galley, and took a cold beer out of the refrigerator. As she took a long swig, her attention was drawn to the pounding and a tremulous voice coming from the master stateroom.

"Kevin? Is that you? Let me out of here. What's going on? Kevin?"

Tia tilted her head toward the noise and took another swig of beer. Showtime. She strolled down the stairs toward the voice. "Step away from the door!" Dead silence followed the order.

"Who are you?" Jody finally responded.

"I said, step away from the door." Tia placed her half-empty bottle on a table. She slid the huge bolt-lock backward, opened the door, and was nearly knocked down by a charging body. She grabbed Jody around the waist with one arm and used her captive's own momentum against her to fling her back through the door. Jody landed on her back on the king-sized bed, the wind almost knocked out of her.

"When I tell you to do something, you damned well better do it. Are we clear on that?"

Jody was stunned. She wasn't a weak woman. She worked out every other day, she went rock climbing once a week, she was in shape; yet she had been tossed around like a hacky sack. A dark-haired woman leaned against the frame. Her tall body silhouetted against the backlighting of the salon gave her an ominous appearance. Jody tried to make out facial features but couldn't. The stranger's strength aside, what concerned Jody even more was the woman's calm. When she found her breath, she said, "Where's Kevin?"

"Kevin's on vacation."

Jody tried to remember whether she had ever heard the voice before. The woman had to be lying about Kevin's whereabouts. She tried to shake away the last remnants of her headache in order to focus. "Who are you?"

"Who I am is not your concern."

Jody blanched. "What do you want?"

"I want you to behave. It's as simple as that. Just do as you're told, don't give me a hard time, don't do anything stupid, and you should be fine." She reached around the corner and when her hand returned to view, it held a beer. She took a drink.

"Are you... did... have I been kidnapped?" Jody's breath caught in her throat; she clearly knew the answer.

Tia's mouth went dry as she studied the young woman who lay on the berth, staring at her. Jody was in the same position she had landed in when Tia threw her back on the bed. The fear blooming in the wide, expressive eyes and the quiver in the voice suddenly had Tia thinking thoughts other than what Montgomery was expecting of her. Alcohol always lowered her restraint. In a different setting, Tia would have been all over this sexy babe, but not here. Not now.

Tia found her voice. "You have been abducted, yes. A ransom will be asked in exchange for your safe return. It's really very simple... as long as the ransom gets paid with no complications, you'll be back in your rich little playground in no time, a little lighter in the bank account but nothing I'm sure you or your parents can't make up for in a few weeks."

"I can't believe it."

"I can't believe it hasn't happened sooner." Tia casually took another swallow.

"How did— How did I get here?" Jody slowly sat up and rested her back against the wall. "How did you know about this yacht?"

"Come on. It's not like you and your family exactly hide yourselves. Every other day, someone from your family tree or elite social circle is on the gossip pages of every newspaper in the world. Your private life is an open book. But then, that's what you get for being famous."

"This is where you're going to keep me until you get paid?"

"I know, right? Poor you, having to be held hostage on a million-dollar boat."

Jody drew her knees up to her chest protectively and hugged them close, resting her head on them. Her voice broke as she asked, "How much are you asking for me?"

"Why? If it's over a certain amount, Mommy and Daddy won't pay?" The antagonism in Tia's voice made it seem as if she was unaffected by the anxiety in Jody's voice. That wasn't true. Something about Jody's bearing and the wounded look on her face caused Tia to want to get drunker to forget what she was doing to an innocent victim.

"No," she said in almost a whisper. "They'll pay it. Just something else Mother can blame me for."

"Whatever. So, before I lock you back in here, are you hungry? Thirsty?"

Jody shook her head without looking up. "No, thank you. There's water in the mini-fridge here… unless you removed that, too."

"No." Tia was surprised to hear her own voice soften. "There's still water and club soda in there."

"Thank you."

As Tia re-secured the door, she heard Jody crying and inexplicably, unexpectedly, the sound tugged at her heart.

Chapter 8

There is nothing consistent about human behavior except its tendency to drift toward evil.
        —Anonymous

When the burn phone rang, Tia answered it on the second ring.
"Where are you?" Montgomery asked.
"The bridge."
"And she's in the master stateroom?"
"Yep."
"How is she?"
"How do you think she is?" Tia sighed into the silence. "Scared. Tearful."
"That's to be expected. But no problems?"
"Nope. Everything has gone as planned."
"Good, good. Okay, well, I'll do my part. The old man will get the notification and ransom request first thing in the morning."
"I suppose you have your strategy for your shocked response all planned out," Tia said. Maybe if she could get more of a handle on Montgomery's thought processes, she could get an idea of how to protect herself.
"Not to worry. As soon as I get back to the estate, I'll start calling around to try and find out where she is because her not being home at this hour is unusual. Of course, no one will know where she is. I'll finally contact her parents to see if she's there, and they'll tell me she's not, which I already know."
"Aren't you concerned they'll grill you in detail about everything?"
"Nah. I'll tell them things were fine at dinner, and when Jody left, she said she might stop by the local pet market to pick up some treats for our menagerie. That's a personal touch they'll believe, because she's a damned fool for those stupid animals."

"You don't like your pets?"

"Maybe if we had pets, but we have an entire Humane Society in our south wing."

"Your house has wings?" Tia rolled her eyes. Figures.

"I told you, we're not exactly poor."

"Well, *she's* not poor," Tia said, knowing that would antagonize him.

"Bite me, Ramone. I do just fine without the Wainwright fortune."

"Of course you do," Tia said dryly. "What else will you tell them to convince them you're not involved?" Sarcasm was dripping from her tone, and she couldn't control it. But if she got him back on their original subject, he would keep talking about his perceived brilliance; talking about himself was clearly something he loved to do.

"I'll tell them I pulled into the garage, and her car wasn't there, and it wasn't parked anywhere in the driveway, either. I'll tell them I asked the staff if they had seen or heard from her and they told me no. I'll tell them I called all her friends, which I will do when I get home, and because it's so late, that will not only rouse everyone's curiosity, it will make me look even more innocent if the police question them. 'Oh, yeah,' they'll say. 'He called us at one in the morning. He was really concerned.'" Montgomery chuckled. "I'll begin calling her cell every fifteen minutes, call the hospitals and police stations to see if she's been in an accident. I'll make sure I tell Wainwright I've done all these things when I wake him up in an hour or so."

"Got it all figured out, I see." He certainly is a calculating son-of-a-bitch, Tia thought.

"No conceivable reason it shouldn't go precisely like that."

"For your sake, I hope it works out like that," Tia said, not meaning it.

"No, for *your* sake, let's hope it works out just like that." Montgomery snickered. "I can just see the expressions on her parents' faces. John will be beside himself, terrified and angry. Jody is his pride and joy. Sondra will be her usual annoyed and indifferent self. You have no idea how much I look forward to watching that glacial bitch's dispassionate, uppity façade finally crack when she realizes her daughter's gone. Of course, it really won't surprise me if Sondra doesn't care."

Tia perked up at that tidbit of information. "Mommy and baby don't get along?"

"Mommy dearest is a mess. Sondra constantly puts herself in competition with Jody, especially when it comes to John's attention and affection. It's as if Jody's responsible for Sondra's personal shortcomings and John's devotion to their daughter. Jody has wasted a lot of time and energy trying to please her mother and gain Sondra's acceptance and respect. It's ridiculous."

So that's what she meant when she said this was something else her mother could blame her for. "Be careful, Montgomery. It almost sounds as if you have feelings for your wife."

He continued as though he hadn't heard her. "Maybe I should have left Jody alone and taken her mother… but then, John might not have agreed to pay the ransom for Sondra. At least not five hundred million dollars."

"Five hundred million? And I'm only getting ten?"

"Be happy I'm cutting you in on any of it, Ramone. Look, I'm hanging up because I'm almost home."

"So, when do you think we can wrap this up?"

"When I get the money."

Tia's throat tightened. "Don't you mean when we get the money?"

"No. I mean when I get the money. I told you, you'll be paid accordingly."

"Right." She wasn't convinced. "And when might that be?"

"Wainwright won't wait too long, and he won't like the FBI running the show, either. If the feds can't find out who or what they're dealing with, I give the old man a week at the most before he takes matters into his own hands and agrees to pay the ransom to get his darling daughter back."

"A week? You've got to be fucking kidding me!"

"It'll take as long as it takes. Relax. When was the last time you got to live like this, anyway? Oh… that's right. Colombia."

Tia was stunned. "How the hell do you know about that?"

"It's a declassified case. It's all public record, if you know where to look. And I did." He sighed. "So let's get back to our fucking little problem child in the master stateroom."

"A minute ago you sounded like you loved her, and now you sound like you really hate her."

"I don't love her, not like I should, given our circumstances. And I don't hate her, either," he said matter-of-factly. "It isn't really about her."

"No, of course not. I forgot. It's about you." She took a deep breath and released it slowly. She needed to know. "So let me ask… you going to kill her?"

"No. You are."

Goddamnitalltohell! "That wasn't in the agreement," Tia said sharply.

"The rules change as I see fit."

"That was not what we agreed to. I'm not going to do it."

"We didn't agree to anything. You don't have a choice. If you had balls—which is in question—I would have you by them, don't forget that. That body in the Expedition has got to be getting pretty ripe by now. It's only a matter of time before it gets discovered. Your fingerprints are everywhere, your DNA is all over her, your bullet is in her heart, and your gun is in the car. What's one more body?"

"I didn't kill her, you did." Tia began to pace.

"Not according to the evidence."

"Why kill your wife? You'll get your money, I'll get mine, and we can all go our merry ways. Killing that hooker was unnecessary, but I can see in your sick mind why you felt you had to do it, and yes, I will be wanted for that murder. But with the amount of money you're going to give me, I know how to vanish. If your wife dies and any of this gets linked to me, it doesn't matter how much money I have or where I go, I'll be looking over my shoulder the rest of my life."

"Not my problem. You're a loser, Ramone. If I hadn't found you and set you up, someone else would have. Now… when the ransom is safely delivered, either you'll kill her, or I'll kill you both."

"How do I know you won't do that anyway?"

"You don't. I guess you'll just have to believe that I won't."

"Yeah. *That'll* happen. I wouldn't believe you if you told me you were lying." She had learned very quickly that there were essentially two reasons why she couldn't trust people: one, because she knew them; and the other, because she didn't. She should have taken Montgomery out when he got into the car with her, even if it had meant running the risk of getting shot. She was going to have to find a way out of this mess with the least amount of damage to herself, and she was going to have to do it soon.

Tia poured another shot as she absorbed the implications of her conversation with the coldhearted prick. She tossed back the drink and let the robust liquor further numb her senses.

"What?" he asked, his tone smug. "No other argument?"

"What's the point? Arguing with you is about as useless as trying to blow out a lightbulb."

"I know you're not going to give up that easily. And don't think of getting cute with me, either, because if I suspect you're doing anything to betray me, I'll set the feds on your tail so fast, you won't know what hit you."

"You're kind of a soulless bastard, aren't you?"

His laugh made her shiver. "As they used to say in grade school, it takes one to know one."

"Are we done?" she asked curtly.

"For now."

Tia snapped the phone shut and tossed it onto one of the sofas, considering whether Jody could have heard her end of the conversation. There were two closed doors and two levels between them, and the hot tub and the stereo were both on. She wasn't sure why she cared—after all, once she got the money, Jody Montgomery really wasn't her concern—but she did care, and she needed to dissect those feelings.

Jody sat on her berth and stared at nothing for a very long time. Kidnapping had always been a possibility; her father had spoken of it often when she was younger. She had lived twenty-eight years without it happening, and she had to admit she had become complacent as, she was sure, had her parents. Her husband brought it up a few times, but he didn't seem concerned that it would ever become a reality. Maybe that was because he knew any kidnappers would most likely contact her parents to pay a ransom; they had the money.

Her guard had made one good point: if she was to be held hostage, there were much worse places than *The Quintessence. Who is this woman and how did she get me to the yacht? And how did she get access to it?* It made Jody shudder to think that something fatal might have happened to Kevin. Surely someone would miss him and come out to check on him. Surely someone would explore every avenue, including the boat, looking for her. *What would happen if they did find me here?* The woman had said that if she played along, everything would be fine. *Can I believe her? Is it only about the money?* Hopefully it was. She would comply with this woman's instructions. There was no need to aggravate her and make the experience any worse.

Aside from the obvious, there was nothing about the woman that should have piqued Jody's interest the way it had. Yet Jody was fascinated by the deep, rich voice, cocky stance, and total air of command. And she was curious as to why the woman had kidnapped her. She couldn't help wanting to know more.

But when the woman came to the door and calmly asked Jody if she needed anything before she settled in for the night, Jody felt a sense of doom.

The first light of day broke at 6:32 a.m. Jody knew this because she was frequently checking the alarm clock. She didn't really trust the stranger who now shared the yacht with her, so she had forced herself to stay awake. She had only dozed twice throughout the night.

She got out of bed, stepped into the head to relieve her bladder, and washed up. She opted not to take a shower, not wanting to be naked and defenseless should her captor barge in on her. During the night, she had noticed that the locks had been reversed on the bathroom door, too. She couldn't lock anyone out, but she could be locked in.

While she waited for contact from her kidnapper, Jody inspected the room and immediately discovered why her bedside lamp and ceiling lights didn't work—the bulbs had been removed, as had any devices that connected to the outside world. Along with the radio, the television that had been attached to the entertainment system was gone. Maybe it was best she didn't hear her father's anguished pleas for her safe return or watch her mother stoically stand by, devoid of any emotion other than indignation.

Jody opened the porthole and put her face up to it. She breathed deeply of the sea air, grateful for the feeling of being alive. She prayed she would live to see another day, prayed her parents and husband would cooperate so that she could go home, and prayed her house staff would feed and tend to her four-legged family in her absence. She was aware Tony couldn't care less about her pets, but she knew Richard, their houseman, and Richard's daughter, Melanie, doted on the furry creatures, so she was certain they would take turns ensuring the animals were taken care of.

She didn't know anything about the woman who had kidnapped her, but her frightening demeanor warned Jody it would be unwise to cross her. What did the woman have against her, or her family, or was she just in it for the money?

She wondered if she would ever find out.

Tia woke in her usual hungover state, nothing a cup of black coffee couldn't remedy. She was aware that coffee as a cure for hangovers was a myth, and all it really did was make someone a wide-awake drunk, but it was a step toward rising out of the haze she was in. Coffee, a cool shower, and a little hair of the dog.

She wished she could just stay in bed. Unfortunately that wasn't an option, and she rolled off the berth in the forward stateroom. It wasn't as luxurious as the room holding her captive, but it was still pretty damned nice, and much more appealing than her residential hotel room at the North Avenue Arms.

The day before, she had moved some of Montgomery's clothes to the room where she would be sleeping until the assignment was over. Since she hadn't been able to pack a suitcase for this little venture, she had sorted through the closet in the master stateroom and selected some items from the sweats, T-shirts, denim shirts, shorts, and beach pants she found there. There was also a windbreaker she had discovered hanging in the port-side stateroom. She wasn't sure who it belonged to; it seemed too feminine for Montgomery and too large for his wife. Whose ever it was, she had adopted it. It came in handy for protection against the mist that rolled in occasionally while she was on the deck at night.

She slipped into a pair of black lounging pants and a tank top, climbed the stairs, and used the head. She moved to the galley, filled the small sink with water and ice cubes, and dunked her face in it. *That* woke her up.

She regarded the coffeemaker, a high-tech, European-looking monster that didn't seem any less complicated to navigate than it had the morning before. Instead she made instant coffee in the microwave. She wanted to head off the disagreeable throbbing in her temples, and the coffee would help. While she waited for that to heat, she rubbed the nagging sting from her eyes and thought about the day ahead of her.

She figured the beep from the microwave would alert Jody that she was up and about, and she wondered whether Jody had gotten any sleep. The young woman hadn't reacted or behaved the way Tia thought she would. Tia had presumed Jody would be a pompous, out-of-touch-with-reality, supreme bitch, a woman who would not take her kidnapping too seriously, knowing her family would pay the ransom because they were all richer than God, a woman who would impatiently consider her captivity an annoyance more than anything else. Tia had expected the very privileged Mrs.

Montgomery to be a handful, to yell and scream and kick at the door all night with a *"Don't you know who I am?"* attitude.

When the heiress responded to her abduction by lying in a fetal position, her voice small and scared and crushed, Tia almost felt sorry for her. If it was an act, the former CIA officer would know soon enough.

Chapter 9

An honest man alters his ideas to fit the truth, and a dishonest man alters the truth to fit his ideas.
—Anonymous

When he wasn't becoming more and more financially obligated to his boss by using steroids to enhance the results of his workouts, Bruce Wechsler programmed computers for MediMont. Though he was self-educated, he was good at what he did. The mechanics of any sort of electronic component, device, or equipment were very easy for him to grasp. He made sure he kept up on new technology as soon as it came out and applied his expertise at every opportunity. He had a natural aptitude for computers and could have a much better paying, more prestigious job if he hadn't hit a few snags along the way.

He was proud that he had pulled himself up from his unprepossessing beginnings as a juvenile delinquent. He had been thrown into jail at sixteen for stealing parts from a friend's father's computer repair shop. After three months in a youth correctional facility, Bruce had no doubts that he didn't like incarceration at all. His redemption lasted ten years.

To impress a woman who worked out at the gym where he was employed part-time, a then scrawny Bruce hooked up with a trainer of less than sterling character. Mitch eased him into bulking up and started Bruce on a course of Dynabol and Drive, steroids recommended for use only with horses, dogs, and cats. When that muscle building combination plateaued and his physique improvement plan stalled, Mitch moved him to Stanazol.

Before Bruce knew it, he was addicted and in debt to his trainer, who cut him off until he could settle his tab. Desperate, Bruce begged Mitch to fix him up. For some reason, Mitch felt sorry for the former juvie offender and hooked Bruce up with his dealer.

The distributor needed some major computer work done and was in search of someone less than ethical to do it. While programming the dealer's system, Bruce found the name of the distributor's wholesaler, and that led him to a prominent businessman, Anthony Montgomery.

Montgomery hired Bruce as a junior programmer and troubleshooter at MediMont. Unrealistically, Bruce had hoped Montgomery was his ticket out of the financial dregs, but every week he got deeper and deeper in debt to his new boss. While Montgomery was generous at setting him up with a more than adequate supply of Anadrol, he didn't pay Bruce enough to afford the nasty habit. If Bruce had known Montgomery had ulterior motives, he might have done what he could to break away. He had begun to think that maintaining his muscle mass wasn't worth the cost.

He took responsibility for his addiction to steroids, and he was faithful about working off his debt to his boss, but he wanted no part of what Montgomery had ordered him to do now. He had only met Mrs. Montgomery one time. She had stopped by the office while he was installing a new inventory program on the boss's computer. She smiled at him, said hi, and dropped off something for her husband. He thought she seemed nice. And that she was gorgeous. That's when he became slightly smitten.

Why Montgomery wanted to terrorize the poor woman just to get even with his father-in-law was beyond Bruce. There had to be ways to take Wainwright down without using Mrs. Montgomery as bait. Bruce had heard rumors that Montgomery was ruthless when it came to competition. Some people had even used the word "sociopath" when describing him. In the time that Bruce had been associated with his boss, he had discovered that two of Montgomery's wholesalers who had attempted to rip him off had "disappeared." This was not an aspect of Montgomery that was advertised around the office and was clearly not the character he showed to his wife and in-laws. That Montgomery was so capable of successfully concealing that side of his personality scared the shit out of Bruce, and fear commanded his allegiance now that he was in the kidnap plot up to his eyeballs. First, he stole the Expedition and rented the Volvo, next, he leased the storage space, and now he was in charge of the ransom calls. If any of it got traced back to him, he was fucked.

As much as Bruce hated his involvement, and despite being nervous as hell, Montgomery terrified him to the point where he didn't dare fail to follow through with the plans. There he sat, ready to make the phone call that would bring the world's attention to the woman who would soon be the most famous kidnapped heiress since Patty Hearst.

Bruce had set up the system to speak using an advanced Text-To-Speech (TTS) program. TTS was computer-generated speech synthesized from tiny fragments that then were glued together and played to the person on the other end of the phone line. So when John Wainwright asked questions, Bruce would type in the answer and the computer would speak it, sounding exactly like a real person. If Jody's father began to get too specifically inquisitive, Bruce would type in an advisory that Wainwright would be contacted with further instructions and the call would be terminated.

For the first call, Bruce would not be concerned with a line trace. The second call would be routed through several relay stations in such a way that it would appear as if it originated in Asia. The next call would trace to Canada, the next to Australia, etc. Bruce was sure that by at least the fourth day, the FBI would know that the calls were coming from somewhere in the United States, and would be able to nail his location in one minute. Thereafter, whatever Montgomery was going to have him say would have to be done in fifty-eight seconds or less, and even that would be cutting it close.

Bruce hoped that in four days the ordeal would be over.

Anthony Montgomery was at the Wainwright estate when the first ransom call came in. He arrived there a little before nine a.m. and frantically delivered his carefully rehearsed speech to Jody's parents—she hadn't come home all night, hadn't called, had basically disappeared off the face of the earth after dinner at The Cypress. He had done everything he could to locate her.

It was hard enough on John Wainwright that his precious daughter was missing, the victim of God-knew-what, but when Montgomery threw in for good measure that their dinner at the Cypress was to celebrate Jody's pregnancy, the billionaire was beside himself, as Montgomery had predicted. The joyous news of a grandchild was overshadowed by the fear that something terrible might have happened to his daughter *and* his future heir.

As expected, Sondra remained her nasty, disdainful self, and sniffed that Jody might have just negligently run out of gas and forgotten to recharge her cell phone battery. Even after Montgomery argued that Jody had never been that irresponsible and it had to be something darker that was going on, Sondra was ready to put the blame for anything sinister happening directly on her daughter's shoulders. Montgomery suspected that Sondra knew that whatever was going on, it probably wasn't good, and all that would do was take John's limited focus off of her. She clearly resented it. Under her breath she muttered about the kidnapping happening with a baby on the way—the eagerly anticipated heir—which would finally put John in a better mood. His constant complaining about the lack of a grandchild had been pushing her over the edge.

Although Montgomery would be responsible for the impending death of his wife, he couldn't help but lash out at her mother's indifference.

"You know, Sondra, you could be a little bit more concerned and a little less self-centered here. Your daughter has vanished. If she had run out of gas, or even driven off the road, she would have gotten word to someone. She's not helpless and she's not stupid, regardless of how you try to make her feel."

Hazel eyes bored through him, punctuating an expression of barely controlled rage. "How dare you! You've only known my daughter a little over three years, and we all know it wasn't true love that got you together. It was money. I've had her in my life for almost twenty-nine years. She's not the perfect little princess you and her father make her out to be." This statement drew a sharp glare from John but he stayed silent. "You don't know her as well as I do."

"You don't know her at all." Montgomery threw the words at his spiteful mother-in-law. That caused him an unexpected flash of guilt, but it left as quickly as it had appeared.

Just then the phone rang. It was ten o'clock. Everything was going exactly as he had planned.

When Wainwright hung up the phone, his face had drained of all color. He hadn't said much; the kidnapper did most of the talking. He looked at his wife—who turned away from him, her face displaying her antipathy—and then to Montgomery, who anxiously drew nearer. They had heard John's end of the conversation, and the content of the message was clear.

"What's happening?" Montgomery asked with as much alarm as he could generate.

"Jody's been kidnapped. She's safe. For now. The bastard will call back tomorrow with a ransom demand. We're not to go to the police."

Montgomery ran his hand through his hair and sighed. "Aw, Christ…"

"What do you think of your revered child now, John? She allowed herself to be kidnapped because she was, no doubt, careless. I wonder how much money her recklessness is going to cost us." Sondra's voice dripped with contempt.

"That's enough!" Wainwright bellowed. "I don't know how you can carry someone inside of you for nine months and conveniently forget she's your child when she's not doing things to make you shine. She *is* your child, too, Sondra, for God's sake. This isn't about you! Our daughter could be murdered. We're not dealing with Jody's occasional lack of grace here. We're dealing with Jody's life!"

Sondra stalked out of the room, her coldness exceeding anything Montgomery had expected from her. He turned back to Wainwright, whose crimson face echoed his assessment. "Jesus Christ, John." Montgomery folded his arms. "What is wrong with her?"

"She doesn't comprehend that this is real. It is probably too much for her to grasp just yet."

"Stop making excuses for her!" Montgomery barked. "Has she always been this indifferent to Jody?" The glacial mask that had frozen Sondra's face the minute she determined from Wainwright's side of the phone conversation that there had, indeed, been an abduction, was downright heartless.

"I can't be bothered with her petty insecurities right now. We need to call the police."

Montgomery smiled inwardly. His father-in-law was so predictable. "Didn't the caller say not to do that?"

"I want my daughter back alive, but if, God forbid, that doesn't happen, I want the FBI already on this bastard's tail!"

"I want my wife back alive, John. I think we should do what he says."

Wainwright pulled his cell phone from the inner pocket of his suit jacket and flipped it open. "He didn't call you to tell you that he had Jody. He's not going to call you for the ransom. So this is my decision."

"Then it's on your conscience if we never get her back," Montgomery told him, bluntly.

Wainwright hesitated, then he dialed 911.

Chapter 10

A lie is the deliberate withholding of any part of the truth from someone who has the right to know.
—Anonymous

Jody knew her captor was up and about; she had heard the beep of the microwave. She wondered when the woman would come to the stateroom, and whether she would be able to find out any more about this woman who had taken her hostage or, at least, the reason why.

She longed for a shower, knowing the spray of water would perk her up, but she didn't dare. Her stomach had started to protest its deprivation, as breakfast was the one meal she tried to never miss. She had drunk a bottle of raspberry-flavored water, but that only made her hungrier. The grumbling from her belly had reached a substantial volume by the time she heard the knock.

"Yes?" Jody wanted to sound stronger, more fearless, but she couldn't muster the energy to pretend.

"I've got some breakfast for you. Step away from the door."

Having learned her lesson the night before, Jody walked back to the bed. "Okay." She heard the bolt slide and her captor entered, a tray balanced on one hand while she closed the door with the other. She set the tray down on the vanity and stepped back.

"I don't know what you usually eat in the morning, but I rustled this up," the woman said in a civil manner.

Jody stepped over to the vanity and surveyed the tray. It held a bowl of Rice Krispies, an eight-ounce glass of milk, two slices of buttered wheat toast, and a cup of horrible looking black coffee. She looked up at her captor, seeing her for the first time in daylight.

Jody caught herself before she gasped. Her kidnapper was striking, even in her obviously unkempt state. "Thank you." She didn't dare to stare at the tall woman, not knowing what might provoke her anger. Jody returned her attention to the tray and reached for the glass of milk. She poured enough into her coffee to turn the color to tan. Now that food was in front of her, her stomach lurched at the thought of eating. The presence of the woman didn't help.

The guard took a couple of steps backward, not bothering to hide her visible assessment of Jody's state. Jody knew she looked like shit because she hadn't slept a wink and her face was puffy from crying. Her eyes started watering at her first sip of the coffee.

"Too strong?"

Jody wondered why the woman cared. "A little." She wanted to spit out the mouthful but reluctantly swallowed; she didn't want to insult her unpredictable abductor. She put the mug back on the tray, picked up a slice of toast, and took a nibble to remove the bitter, acidy aftertaste of the coffee. There was no way that sludge had come from her coffeemaker. Jody looked down at the contents of her tray. "Can I ask you something?"

The woman leaned against the door frame and folded her arms. "You can ask anything you want. I won't guarantee I'll answer."

"Why?" Jody looked over at her, and for the first time, their eyes connected. What she saw in those unique amber eyes rattled her. They seemed vacant, devoid of life. The woman held her gaze and openly studied her.

Jody was a little jarred by the woman's smoldering beauty, a physicality that was unexpected; in her sheltered upbringing, she incorrectly assumed that all criminals were male, conspicuous, and never very attractive. There was no doubt her captor had an edge and, obviously, less than pure motives. Jody puzzled over what must have happened to this woman in her life to elicit this kind of behavior from her.

"Well... I could say 'money,' but..."

Jody looked away first as she found the mesmerizing eyes that stared into the depths of her fear too intense. "If it's money you want, if that's what it will take to get me out of here, I can give that to you right now. I can have money transferred anywhere in the world for you *right now*. We don't have to do this." She concentrated on the contents of her tray, her distress outweighing her hunger.

"It doesn't work that way."

Jody returned her focus to her captor. "Why? Why can't it work that way? Let me give you the money, and we can both walk away right now." Her tone was pleading. She took a small step toward the woman. "Please... everybody has a price..."

The woman abandoned her casual stance and moved closer. Her body assumed a menacing posture, clearly not because she had anything to physically fear from the smaller Jody, but the unmistakable warning she sent with subtle body language did the trick.

Immediately realizing her mistake, Jody stopped dead in her tracks. She stepped back and looked down at the floor, but not before she saw that her unspoken submission prompted the woman's mouth to curl into a smile.

"Even if that was an offer that interested me, which it doesn't, it's too late. The first phone call has already been made to your father."

Jody's shoulders slumped in defeat, and her hand covered her eyes. "My parents know I've been kidnapped?"

"Abducted," the woman said. "When an adult is the victim, it's usually referred to as an abduction."

"I'm talking about my life, and you're correcting my phraseology?"

The woman stifled a laugh as she put her hand on the door handle, stopping when Jody spoke again.

"Are you working alone?"

The woman's eyes swept the stateroom before lighting on Jody. "Does it really matter?"

The phrasing rattled Jody for some reason beyond just dread. She cast her eyes downward in embarrassment and mumbled, "No. I guess it doesn't."

"Need anything before I lock you in again?"

"My freedom?"

Before the door swung shut, she heard, "You can't always get what you want, Mrs. Montgomery."

Troubled by her physical reaction to Jody, Tia jogged up the steps to the salon and poured herself a shot of scotch. She couldn't get away from the stateroom fast enough, away from whatever was eliciting the gnawing at her libido.

Regardless of Jody Montgomery's emotional state, she was indisputably pretty, and disarming in her confusion. Tia was drawn to her, a sudden sexual pull that was undeniable. That was not good.

Under different circumstances, Jody would have been a tasty conquest. What a stupid time for her hormones to wake up and stand at attention. She drank another shot and went back up to the deck to wait for the scheduled check-in call from Montgomery.

"How's the lovely Mrs. Montgomery this morning?"

Tia gritted her teeth. She wished she could reach through the phone and grab Montgomery by his throat and squeeze. Her contempt was clear in her voice. "How do you think she is?"

"What's the matter? Get up on the wrong side of my wife this morning?"

Tia knew from the salacious tone of Montgomery's voice that the thought of her screwing his wife most likely made him hard. "Shut up, you sick fuck."

"Jody is a very attractive woman. Don't tell me you haven't thought about it."

"I haven't thought about it." She knew he was fantasizing about it, and the idea of him imagining her in any sexual manner nauseated her.

"Liar."

"Do you have anything to tell me or not? If you don't, I have a beer calling my name."

"This early? My... you're nothing if not dedicated."

Montgomery's inflection was snide. It didn't win him any points with Tia.

"Breakfast of champions. Tell you what, I'll drink to your health, how's that?"

"I'll be sure to be extra careful then. I bet you drink to the health of so many people that your bar tab could be a deductible on your medical insurance."

She started to pace. She hated this man, what he was doing, and what he expected of her. "Did you make the call?"

"Me? No. But the call was made. I was there when it came in. I was appropriately frenzied and distraught. I should have been an actor."

"So what happens now?" She could figure it out for herself. The police would contact the FBI, who would set up a command post at the estate and the crush would be on. The reporter on the cop beat would leak the story to the press, and within an hour, everybody in the world would know what Jody Montgomery looked like.

"I'm waiting on the cops now. The chief of detectives wasn't good enough for my father-in-law. He demanded the police commissioner accompany the feds when they come." His tone was now casual, playful, and Tia found that repugnant. "Oh, by the way… the dead hooker was found this morning."

"Her name was Roxi," Tia said. She recalled the redhead's lifeless expression, and her stomach roiled.

"I know that. I fucked her enough times." He made an audible yawn. Tia shook her head, not able to take in the prick's remorseless attitude. "I give the cops about twenty-four hours before they're on your trail. Fortunately for you, my wife's abduction will take precedence over a discredited ex-CIA dyke murdering her prostitute lover in a stolen car."

It took every ounce of willpower she had to not explode. Until that moment, she had no idea that she was capable of such self-control. "How could a woman as nice as your wife seems to be, have married such a psycho?"

Montgomery let loose a hearty laugh. "I told you—I should have been an actor. Back to business. At some point, the FBI is going to want to check *The Quintessence*, just to make sure Jody hasn't flipped out and run away on her own. When that happens, I'll let you know before we leave the house."

Tia immediately began to sweat. "You're going to bring them *here*?"

"Oh, absolutely. I told you, I've thought of everything. I, of course, will stay on the bridge when they do their walk-through, as it will be too painful for me to go with them, considering all the great times my wife and I have had there… which have been none, but they don't need to know that."

"And where, exactly, will your wife and I be?"

Tia returned to the master stateroom much sooner than she had thought she would. It had only been a matter of minutes since she had left. She once again instructed Jody to step away from the door, and when Jody did, Tia entered with a purpose. As she strode directly toward Jody, the frightened woman instinctively backed away from her.

"Come here," Tia commanded. She reached out and grabbed Jody's forearm. Tia forced herself to look hostile. Jody appeared to be torn between complying and trying to fight.

"Wait! What—"

Jody dug her heels into the carpet in an attempt to resist the pull, but Tia yanked her over to the head. She pushed her inside, shut the door, and secured it.

"What's going on? What did I do?" There was an edge of hysteria in Jody's voice. She slapped her palms against the door. "Please! If these are going to be my last few moments of life, I want to know why."

Ignoring her, Tia moved back over to the berth, where she dropped to her hands and knees. She completely removed one of the drawers underneath the bed and studied its width. She assessed the height of the space and estimated what would be the highest part of her prone body. She didn't want to leave anything to chance, so she lay down and eased her body into the vacant space. It was snug, but she fit. She slid out, stood up, and walked to the other side of the berth. That drawer she removed was the same size as the first one, and that meant the space in between the two drawers would be just about big enough for two people. She stood up and placed her hands on her hips in reluctant admiration. Damned if Montgomery hadn't thought of everything.

Tia put the two drawers back, unlocked the door to the head, and opened it. Jody was seated on the edge of the tub, her arms crossed and her expression reflecting anger, bewilderment, and fear. Tia almost felt guilty. She turned her face away, rolled her eyes, and looked back at Jody. "Come on out," she said calmly.

Jody remained in the same position, tears glistening in her eyes, still obviously apprehensive. "Why did you do that?"

"You don't need to know. Come on out of there."

"No." There was a defiant edge to Jody's voice and a mutinous demeanor that showed Tia there might be some spunk in her after all. "I'm cooperating with you, and I intend to continue cooperating with you. You said if I behaved, everything would be fine. There was no need for you to do what you just did. If you had asked me to go into the head and stay there until you did what you had to do, I would have done it. You don't need to bully me." Jody seemed overcome with frustration as the tears rolled down her cheeks.

Tia sighed as she glanced at her. "You're right. I'm sorry. I was pissed off and I took it out on you. You didn't deserve it."

The apology apparently surprised Jody, who wiped at her tears with the back of her wrist. She slowly stood up, walked past Tia in the doorway, and moved to the vanity. Jody turned toward Tia, who was feeling uncomfortable about the apology. "Can I at least ask your name?"

Tia's first reaction was to tell her it was none of her business, but she couldn't come up with a legitimate reason why Jody shouldn't know. After all, what difference did it make if Jody knew her identity? They both might very well be dead in a couple of days. "It's Tia."

"Tia," Jody repeated. "It sounds… exotic, which seems appropriate. Is that a nickname for anything?"

"No. It's just Tia." She was bemused by Jody's attempt at small talk.

"I'm sure I don't need to tell you my name."

"No, Jody, you don't." Tia relaxed at the sound of her own voice saying her captive's name. She suddenly imagined that name uttered from her lips under entirely different circumstances, and a wave of heat washed over her body. She was sure Jody noticed the flush that rose to her hairline. Once again, she felt the need to bolt. She picked up Jody's breakfast tray and walked to the door.

"Tia?"

She stopped but didn't turn around. "Yes?"

"Can you stay longer and talk to me?" Jody sounded needy.

Tia very much wanted to. She wanted to get to know her captive on a more personal level, wanted to look at her lovely face for a few unguarded moments. Tia was entranced like she hadn't been since, well, Colombia. She wanted some of Jody's decency and decorum to rub off on her, wanted Jody to make a difference. She wanted Jody to liberate her from herself, a task she considered impossible; she wouldn't have placed that burden on anyone. "I don't think that's such a good idea."

She locked Jody in and headed for the bridge. She needed a drink. Badly.

Chapter 11

One of the most painful wounds in the world is a stab of conscience.
—Rabbi Schlomo Price

Jody sat on the king-sized berth, staring at nothing and thinking about how she had come to be thrust into a living nightmare. She was being held for ransom by whoever this Tia person and her silent partner were, knowing her father would do whatever it took to get her back, knowing her mother would hold this against her for the rest of her life—if she even survived—and knowing her husband would be caught in the middle. If there had ever been any chance of her living in relative anonymity, it would be gone now.

The idea that she might be dead within the next couple of days felt surreal. Evidently there was no rationalizing with her captor; even more evident, money wasn't the real reason Jody was being held hostage. Tia had to know that Jody could make good on her proposition to buy her way out of the situation, yet her offer had been immediately rebuffed. The emptiness in the woman's eyes reflected a barren soul, which Jody interpreted as a lack of conscience. If that were true, she suspected Tia could, and no doubt would, kill her should something go wrong. She could only hope that the plan was not to eliminate her regardless of whether or not the ransom was delivered.

And yet, this woman—her kidnapper, her abductor—had her riveted. Had she actually seen a small spark of something in Tia's eyes when she apologized? Jody wanted to know more about Tia, what made her tick, why she was doing what she was doing. There had to be a story behind her actions, an explanation that justified her criminal behavior. Maybe if Jody could appeal to that, make Tia see her as more than just an object, Tia would think twice about harming her.

Jody turned her focus to her yacht. How had Tia gained access to it? The location wasn't a secret, but neither was it well publicized. Finding it wouldn't have been difficult, but Kevin never would have allowed anyone access without clearing it through her or Tony first. Was the young security officer in on the abduction? She supposed it was possible, but she didn't believe it. Kevin had been in their employ for three years, and his loyalty was beyond question.

Had this woman and her partner ambushed him, too, and disposed of him? That was just too horrible for her brain to wrap around, that she could indirectly be responsible for Kevin's death. Without evidence to the contrary, she would choose to believe he actually was on vacation.

Her attention went back to the glass of milk on her vanity. She thought about the breakfast she should have been eating: Eggs Florentine, vanilla yogurt with fresh raspberries, seven-grain toast, and a latte with a hint of caramel. She thought about what she should have been doing that day—volunteering at the South Shore Animal Shelter in the morning and telling stories to the kids in the pediatric cancer ward at South Shore Hospital in the afternoon. Although she felt emotionally rewarded by both activities, they were also heartbreaking and had begun to take a toll on her natural optimism.

She had been pretty successful at finding homes for the animals who weren't too severely injured, but having to watch more and more abused pets come in on a daily basis had begun to test her resolve. She was of the opinion that anyone who harmed an animal should have the same thing done to them as punishment.

Then there were the kids. She was getting too attached to the brave children whose fate was out of her control. She could donate all the money in her bank account, and it wouldn't cure the patients in the oncology unit. The research her money funded might help future cancer patients, but not the current group. However, the time she donated was rewarding and the kids had given her much more than she could ever give to them. It was these children who taught her that the greatest wealth was being content with little, a lesson she wished her mother had learned.

Dismissing her introspection, Jody stood up and began to pace again. When would her next encounter with Tia take place?

Stretched out on the deck, Tia soaked up the heat of the sun as it toasted her skin. Her can of Sapporo was tepid, though she considered it alcohol abuse to allow beer to get piss warm. She rubbed her eyes with the back of her hand and contemplated her predicament. She was being framed for a murder she didn't commit and was being set up for another murder that had yet to be committed. Whether or not she actually killed Montgomery's wife wasn't the point; Montgomery had made it very clear that, one way or another, Jody was going to end up dead. The question was why?

Tia couldn't come up with justification for Montgomery to want the fetching woman dead. If the ransoming went off without a hitch, Jody could be returned to her family with no one the wiser about her husband's involvement. Other than pure malevolence on his part, there was no need to eliminate Jody, and that had Tia tied up in knots. Dispatching bad guys served a purpose; murdering the innocent did not.

Tia had no doubt that Montgomery would follow through with killing her if she didn't get rid of his wife. Montgomery was also smart enough to leave no witnesses to his part in the abduction and would undoubtedly execute her and this Bruce guy, too, whether or not she did his bidding. If she could find an angle, a way out of this mess, nobody had to die, including herself.

This was about self-preservation, but if she was going to get herself out of this situation without dying, she might as well rescue Jody as well. But how? She was in deep, but was it such an abyss that she couldn't climb out? Every problem had a solution. She just had to figure out what it was.

Chapter 12

No amount of riches can atone for poverty of character.
—Anonymous

Sondra Wainwright watched as the FBI set up their intricate technical trapping devices. While she played the dignified, overwrought mother, she silently seethed at all the activity that invaded her home. Damn her daughter! The focus was supposed to have been on her this week. She had been scheduled to receive an award from the Metro Beach Arts Council for her relentless fundraising that had netted the organization close to a million dollars. It was a big deal. Her fifteenth fundraising award in two years, the event was to have been covered by the media, and that would have been a distinction that separated her from everyone else in her social group.

And now it was going to be overshadowed by this. Once again, her dear Jody had stolen her thunder, and Sondra was quite sure she would never have the spotlight again. She watched her husband and son-in-law interact with the federal agents in the sitting room, and she tried to stay out of the way of the other worker bees as they set up their equipment.

She simmered in self-pity. When a female agent asked her if she was okay and assured her that they would do everything possible to get her daughter back, Sondra bristled. She didn't care if they ever got Jody back. That girl was nothing but an obstacle in her path to being first in her husband's affections and foremost at embellishing the respected Wainwright name.

Jody's charity work was noble, and she was highly praised for it in bourgeois circles, but she never quite grasped the concept of her aristocracy. Sondra never understood how a daughter of hers could have turned out to be the exact opposite of what she always wanted and expected of her. All the private schools, tutors, and training with the best of the best hadn't had the desired impact on the inherently kindhearted and ridiculously benevolent heiress. Try as she might, the supercilious Mrs. Wainwright had not turned Jody into a snob. In her eyes, her daughter was useless, an embarrassment.

She'd never wanted a child and had only agreed because producing an heir was a provision of her prenuptial agreement. John needed someone to whom to pass his fortune and legacy. Sondra despised every day of her pregnancy, cursing it for what it did to her perfect figure for six of those nine months, and hating every second of her seventeen hours of labor. When Jody was born, she was immediately placed in the care of nurses and nannies. The only time Sondra spent "quality" time with Jody was when John insisted or when she was competing for John's time and attention or when a family outing was going to be covered by the press.

The child might have walked on water as far as John was concerned, but Sondra made sure Jody knew she never quite lived up to her mother's standards. She never really liked the little brat, but Jody never seemed to grasp the truth that regardless of how hard she tried, nothing she did would ever change how her mother felt about her.

If Sondra hadn't known better, she would have suspected her daughter had arranged her own kidnapping. She knew, however, that Jody would never have put her father through the trauma, especially not with a Wainwright heir on the way. The pregnancy was something else to raise Jody up a notch in John's eyes, pushing Sondra even further out of the picture. Sondra reached for the decanter of bourbon, oblivious to how much of her bitterness and resentment showed in her body language.

His mother-in-law's aggravation didn't escape Anthony Montgomery. Maybe he should have set up Sondra to take the fall for Jody's death. Would have served the bitch right.

The Wainwright residence was in barely controlled chaos. Uniforms and ill-fitting suits were everywhere, as were cables and wires and computers and federal technicians. The personnel milling around included members of the Critical Incident Response Team, a group expressly assembled to deploy a staff of specialists trained in areas of negotiation, communications, and behavioral sciences and to provide command logistical support. The local Police Tactical Response Squad was also in attendance, their best behavior assured by the presence of the police commissioner, a personal friend of John Wainwright.

House staff busied themselves serving the official "guests" while privileged friends and business associates were allowed into the inner sanctum, much to the dismay of the FBI. Montgomery heard, "I'm so sorry, Tony," and "Don't worry, they'll get her back," so many times, he thought he'd retch if he heard it once more. Yet each time, he would nod somberly and pat the hand of the person grasping his arm or shoulder. When a concerned colleague of his father-in-law's headed toward him for the fourth time, looking more dour than the last, Montgomery excused himself and made a beeline for the exterior patio off the living room. He approached the official-looking young man who was on a cigarette break.

Montgomery engaged in small talk with the agent, who seemed uncomfortable to be standing there exchanging pleasantries with the man whose wife was missing. Montgomery tried his damnedest to look like a man who was beside himself with despair.

Finally Agent Danny Marciano said, "I don't want you to worry, Mr. Montgomery. We're very good at what we do, and we'll do everything we can to make sure Mrs. Montgomery is returned to you safely."

"How many kidnappings have you handled?"

"Well..." The agent looked out over the vast landscape, avoiding direct eye contact with Montgomery. "This is actually my first."

"And what about the rest of your team?"

"Agent Sanborn has supervised three incidents, all with successful results."

"I'm thankful to see you guys jumped right on this. Don't you usually have to wait a day?"

"We used to have to wait twenty-four hours before beginning an investigation into an unwitnessed abduction, but experience has shown us those delays can prove fatal for the victim. How we respond in the hours following the abduction is critical."

"And this has nothing to do with her being from one of the world's richest families?"

"I think that also sped things up," Marciano admitted.

"Look, the guy told my father-in-law he didn't want the cops involved, yet here you guys are. What are the odds that's going to piss this guy off enough that he'll hurt my wife?"

"I'm sure the perpetrator anticipated the authorities being called in."

"But what if he didn't?" Montgomery feigned distress.

"Mr. Montgomery, let's not jump the gun here," Marciano said kindly. "Your father-in-law did the right thing. The only way we're going to catch the person behind this is if we get on it right away. We need to make sure your wife actually has been abducted, and that she isn't already…"

Montgomery made sure he looked stricken. "Isn't already what? Dead? Is that what you were going to say?" He sounded as if he was very close to becoming unhinged.

"Sir, listen to me, please," Marciano said calmly. "I'm not trying to be cold here. I understand we're talking about your wife's safety. I would be inconsolable if it were my wife going through this, regardless of the outcome. But before your father-in-law goes any further in his dealings with this abductor, we need a show of good faith. We need to make sure he, or they, actually have your wife, and that she is still alive and not harmed."

Montgomery made a show of reining in his emotions. "Of course. That makes sense."

Proof of life was already in his plan. He would call Tia with a script of what he wanted Jody to say, as well as the headlines from the morning paper so that the feds would know that she was still alive. Tia would then call Bruce, who would incorporate Jody's monologue into his own computer-processed-voice responses.

"How do you guys orchestrate a ransom payment?" Tony asked.

Marciano sighed. "Mr. Montgomery, the FBI strongly urges private citizens not to pay a ransom."

"Excuse me? This bastard told my father-in-law that he was going to call back tomorrow with a ransom demand. If John refuses to pay the ransom, my wife is as good as dead."

"Sir," Marciano said patiently, "the FBI cannot participate in establishing or enforcing a ransom strategy. If Mr. Wainwright wishes to follow a path that deviates from our hostage resolution policy, he will do it without the consent or cooperation of the Bureau."

"So what you're telling me is that any payment of money or supervision of the transaction is the sole responsibility of the victim's family?"

"That's what I'm telling you. We can be discreetly kept informed of the progress, if that's the route Mr. Wainwright decides to take, but legally, we can't be involved."

Montgomery glanced toward the living room at all the activity, sighed, and ran a well-manicured hand through his expensively styled hair. "God. I know all these people are necessary, but I hope my father-in-law hasn't signed my wife's death warrant by getting you all involved."

"I do appreciate your concern, sir, but, with all due respect, this is what we do."

"Now that you're here, what happens next?"

"We wait for the next call. Although we follow a certain protocol, this kind of investigation is fluid. How we respond will depend on the demands of the abductor. In the meantime, I want to assure you that we are not sitting idle. There are police officers and agents retracing Mrs. Montgomery's last route, looking for leads. Hopefully someone will have witnessed something and will come forward so we can at least get started with a composite drawing. We have helicopters searching for her vehicle, and we have dogs that will track your wife's scent, starting at the last known place she was seen. We have technicians who will be searching the Violent Crime Information Network, which keeps track of crimes and offenders such as convicted kidnappers, registered sex offenders—"

"Oh shit. Oh no! That never even entered my head. Do you think she could be sexually assaulted?" Montgomery asked, panic in his voice.

"I can't predict that, sir. In the case files I've read, abductors are not usually sex offenders. I was just advising you of the contents of the VCIN. I didn't mean to imply anything."

Montgomery put up a hand to halt Marciano's backpedalling. "No, no, it's okay. I just hadn't thought about that aspect. Please go on."

"Are you sure you don't want to talk to the field supervisor or our profiler?"

"Actually, Agent Marciano, I feel comfortable with you, if you don't mind. I'd like to know what the Bureau is going to do to get my wife back to me alive."

Jody watched her captor place the lunch tray on the vanity. Tia was clearly well on her way to being drunk. She didn't act like she was intoxicated, but she smelled like a brewery. She didn't look at Jody once while she was in the room; that bothered Jody a lot.

Jody wanted to ask Tia to join her for lunch, to sit and talk with her while she ate. She was desperate to learn more about this woman, especially about what drove Tia to be inebriated before noon. Since her abductor's temperament was unpredictable, at best, Jody chose to not test her boundaries.

"Is there anything else I can get for you?" Tia asked.

"No, thank you," Jody replied politely.

"I'll be back for the tray later." Tia closed and locked the door behind her.

Jody sighed as she assessed the meal. It was a microwaved container of vegetable lasagna that actually smelled pretty darned good. Her stomach had settled down since that morning, and the aroma wafting up made her hungry. If she didn't eat, she would only be hurting herself, so she picked up the fork and took a tentative bite.

Tia had noted that Montgomery had stocked the yacht with enough food and alcohol to last a full week. He had obviously guessed that she was far from a gourmet cook, as the majority of the provisions were quick and easy to prepare. Tia was fine with that arrangement. If she were to eat anything at all during her binges, she could certainly manage to heat a Marie Callender's frozen entrée. And if it was good enough for her, it was good enough for Jody Montgomery.

Jody. Thinking of her drove Tia to reach for the scotch bottle. It wasn't that Tia didn't like the woman; she liked her too much. She wanted to stay in that cabin and talk to the petite woman, to absorb her. She wanted to tell her not to worry, she would think of something to get them out of this mess; but she hadn't yet come up with any brilliant ideas.

Tia smiled, knocked back the shot and chased it down with another ice-cold beer. She liked the idea of rescuing Jody. Maybe there was hope for her yet.

Chapter 13

Zeal without knowledge is like heat without light.
—English Proverb

The media were gathering outside the gates of the Wainwright estate, setting up their video production and uplink satellite trucks. Network news helicopters buzzed over the area like a swarm of bees. So far, the only thing that had been leaked to the news agencies was that Jody was missing. Until a ransom demand was made and the authorities received a show of good faith, they wanted to limit the information funneled to the public.

Speculation already ran rampant, and it was rumored there had been a kidnapping. When the official announcement was made, the cutthroat rivalry would begin to see who could get the first interview with a family member. Their interest wasn't in Jody Montgomery, or whether their broadcasts might help find her safe and sound, it was about ratings.

"Agent Sanborn," Montgomery said, "why have you decided to alert the press, when the man who called didn't even want the police to know? That seems unreasonably dangerous to me."

The CIRT supervisor viewed Montgomery with an experienced eye. "At this stage of the investigation, sir, your wife is technically missing. The abduction has not yet been substantiated. Allowing the public access to a limited amount of information is an essential tactic in an ongoing search. We hope that keeping your wife in the public eye will result in valid leads that will put us on the trail of the abductor.

"Time is of the essence. Sitting around waiting for the abductor to run the show is not in Mrs. Montgomery's best interests. You never know what someone might have seen after she left you at dinner," Special Agent Sanborn said.

"But doesn't that open you up to all kinds of nutcases? And wouldn't it just take up more of your time to sort through what's an authentic lead and what isn't?" Montgomery asked.

"We'll only release limited information. One of our strategies is to use daily press conferences to let the abductor know we have specific evidence that will lead to him, while holding other things back. That way, when you have the nutcases, as you put it, coming forward with concocted clues and stories, or jumping up and screaming, 'I did it,' we have a way to separate the liars from the credible witnesses or someone actually involved in the case."

"And what if it's an inside job? You know, staff or someone who knew Jody."

Sanborn scratched his chin. "Like a family member?"

"But her only family is her parents and me. John and Sondra have no siblings, John's parents are deceased, and Sondra's parents live very comfortably in Hawaii. And I love my wife very much and have unlimited access to her bank accounts, so it would make no sense for me to ask a ransom for her."

"True. But you'd be surprised at what we see. In any case, everyone in this household, and in yours, will be given a polygraph... just for the purpose of elimination. Should something suspicious come up during that, we'll go from there."

"Isn't a lie detector test inadmissible in court?"

"Honestly, Mr. Montgomery, I'm not concerned with whether or not polygraph results are allowed in court. It's an effective tool to move the investigation forward more quickly. We have one of our top FBI polygraphers flying in today from Washington. He'll start with immediate family and branch out from there—friends, acquaintances, and employees. If anyone has anything to hide, it will come out."

"Well, just let me know when you need me to take mine. I'll do anything to help." He wasn't worried. He'd passed polygraphs before, lying through his teeth. This time should be no different.

"Thank you. Your cooperation is much appreciated. Oh, by the way, you don't have a problem with us taking a look at your personal and work computers, do you?"

"Uh... no, no, of course not, but why is that necessary?" He tried to sound more curious than concerned.

"There's always a possibility that whatever is on Mrs. Montgomery's computer could give us a clue to her whereabouts. With you, it's just a precaution. If you pass the polygraph, we probably won't have to dump your computer, but if your results come up inconclusive, it's just another procedure to help establish your noninvolvement."

Uh oh. Montgomery swallowed hard. *Why didn't I think of that?*

Montgomery was on his way home. It took a police escort to get him off of his in-law's estate without being mobbed by the press. When it looked as if the paparazzi had given up following him, the escort dropped away. Now he was being followed by a single news van that appeared out of nowhere after the cops left. It was four cars behind him in traffic. He didn't care; he had no intentions of going anywhere he shouldn't or behaving in a suspicious manner.

Once he got inside his electronic gates and was safely on his own property, the newshounds were going to get awfully bored if they waited for him to show himself again. He wasn't leaving the haven of his home unless requested to do so by the FBI. There was no need. He had someone else to run his errands. He called Bruce from the car.

"I don't give a good goddamn how you do it, Bruce, but do it! Copy everything off the computer in my office and then send the fucking thing a virus that will crash the machine and destroy everything on the hard drive! Just do whatever the hell it is you do to permanently get rid of that shit!"

"But Tony, that won't guarantee—"

"Just do it, and do it right now!"

As Montgomery passed the rest stop where Jody had been abducted, he saw three uniformed police officers showing flyers and taking notes. It was a popular area for commuters to pull over and take a break or make a pit stop. The possibility was slim that the officers might find anyone who had been there the night before.

"Yes, sir, I'm on it," Bruce replied, immediately hearing the beep on the other end of the line that indicated the call was over. He shut the prepaid wireless phone his boss had provided him for them to communicate during the abduction. Well, if he had to get mired deeper and deeper in this mess, at least Montgomery had finally assigned him a task at which he was good.

If Bruce wanted to, he could disarm the firewalls and antivirus protection, and open up security holes right from his desk. His know-how enabled him to attack anywhere he chose with little chance of detection. But that risked leaving information on the hard drive that any FBI techie could probably retrieve with no problem. He could reformat the drive but decided that would be useless in this case. Repartitioning the drive would only be a little better. That would modify the partition tables stored on the disk but leave the file data on the hard drive intact.

The only way to ensure that all information would be erased would be to use an encryption program to scramble the data, delete it, and then completely overwrite each and every subdivision on the disk. He could do that by repeatedly using fabricated data of configurations with random patterns of ones and zeros. And he had just the disk sanitizing programs to accomplish that.

When all pertinent files had been copied, and everything had been wiped down to the hardware, Bruce would reinstall all the business-related programs to make the system appear normal. If the geeks at the Bureau were able to find anything on Montgomery's computer, it should take them a few years to do it.

Bruce armed himself with a portable file box full of blank and programmed CDs and headed out of his basement office and up to the executive suite. He had his work cut out for him. When this thing was over, if he survived, he had to get a life.

Wanting to see what was being reported about the discovery of Roxi's body, Tia turned the television on. Before she could switch to a local station, she saw a breaking news banner: "Pregnant Heiress Missing." The ex-operative nearly dropped her bottle of beer. The bastard hadn't said anything about his wife being pregnant. If she had ever seriously considered getting rid of Jody, that little tidbit cemented Tia's decision to keep Jody alive. She turned up the volume, and as the unanimated Barbie doll reporter's collagen-injected lips moved, Tia listened with interest.

"... the FBI is not releasing much information at this point in time, but our police source tells us that Joanne Wainwright Montgomery was last seen at approximately eight-thirty last night, leaving The Cypress restaurant, where she and her husband, MediMont mogul Anthony Montgomery, had dinner. Mrs. Montgomery's usual route from the restaurant to the Montgomery home was Dillon Highway." A snapshot flashed across the screen—Montgomery and Jody, both looking happy. God, Tia thought, she certainly is gorgeous.

File footage of a Mercedes the same color and model as Jody's was shown while a voiceover provided a detailed description of the car. Another candid photo of Jody was displayed, and Jody's height, weight, and description were given.

"The family is asking anyone who has seen Joanne Montgomery, or this vehicle, to please come forward. A toll-free tip line is being activated, but until we have that number, please contact your local law enforcement agency or FBI office with any information," the reporter said.

Tia heard the same breaking news several times before she shut off the TV. Only once did the news anchor comment that the mysterious disappearance of the heiress was doubly unfortunate because she was carrying a Wainwright heir. Tia tossed the remote onto the sofa beside her. She needed to talk to Jody Montgomery.

Chapter 14

We underrate that which we do not possess.
—Anonymous

Despite desperately fighting sleep, Jody dozed off after her meal. She stretched out on the bed to rest, was only going to close her eyes for a second, and ended up in a light nap. Something roused her out of her brief siesta, and when she opened her eyes, she bolted upright, startled to find Tia observing her from beside the hot tub.

The look on her face was puzzling. Her expression was not one of menace or intimidation, but of… Did she actually see concern?

"Did you want something?" Jody asked cautiously.

"Actually, I need to ask you something. Are you pregnant?"

The question surprised Jody and momentarily left her speechless. Where had Tia gotten that idea? "No. I'm not. Why?"

"The media seem to think you are," Tia said. "They're referring to you as 'The Pregnant Heiress.' Why would they do that if you're not?"

Jody shook her head again. "I honestly have no idea. Maybe… maybe that's something my parents put out there to make you think twice about harming me."

Tia nodded then shrugged. "Maybe." She straightened up, as if to leave.

Jody looked up at her through honey-colored eyelashes. "Did it work?"

"Did what work?" Tia asked.

"Did it make you think twice about harming me?"

Tia's lips pursed into a smirk, but she remained silent as she left the room and locked Jody inside.

The sultry expression on Tia's face had caused Jody's heart to race, and not in an unpleasant way. She stared at the closed door.

This certainly was an alien feeling. What caused her body to suddenly react as though her insides had just fallen to the bottom of her feet? It must be nerves.

Leaning against the wall outside the master stateroom, Tia closed her eyes. She was relieved that Jody wasn't pregnant, as that would have turned her homicidal toward Montgomery. Him wanting to eliminate his guiltless wife was bad enough, but him wanting to dispose of her *and* their unborn child would have indicated a monster of a whole different caliber.

Not that she didn't think Montgomery had it in him, but if he had known Jody was pregnant and expected Tia to kill her anyway, that would have provoked her to take whatever murder weapon she was supposed to use on Jody and turn it on him instead, and damn the consequences. She speculated on whether she should do that anyway, if she got the chance.

Tia slowly ascended the few steps to the salon, her head swirling with too many thoughts at once, the most preeminent being her libidinous feelings toward her captive. Tia wondered whether Jody was actually being flirtatious or if it was just wishful thinking on her own part. She had to keep things in perspective. Her growing attraction to the younger woman was futile. Jody would never be interested in someone like her, even if Jody was inclined toward the fairer sex. Maybe once upon a time there might have been a chance of something between them but not with the way she was now.

Tia went to the galley for something to eat. She found few possibilities that appealed to her and settled for a bag of corn chips. Back in the salon, she picked up the remote and flopped down on the sofa, all the while replaying Jody's coquettish behavior in her head. She was pretty sure she had read something into it that wasn't intended. Jody was a married woman. Her taste in men left a lot to be desired, but all indications pointed to Jody being straight.

She speculated that even if Jody was remotely interested in women, in her, their interaction had been minimal and certainly not under circumstances conducive to anything other than fear and dislike. And if how they met had been different? Tia wasn't even sure she could do romance anymore. The idea of settling in with a lover who actually meant something was difficult. Ever since Colombia, women had been nothing but sex objects to her. She treated them worse than most men did. Fuck 'em and leave 'em. Anything else was unfathomable to her. Until now.

How could Montgomery have such a gift and not appreciate her? He had a beautiful and, probably, loyal woman in his life and in his bed, and he took that for granted, a display of arrogance that was disgusting. Her hatred for Montgomery took on an entirely different degree of potency.

Not that it mattered. Daydreaming about Jody was frustrating and futile. Mrs. Montgomery was a fantasy, and Tia might as well resign herself to keeping her focus on the task of getting them both out of their situation alive.

She turned the television on and tuned in to a cable news program. It was showing footage of Montgomery as he left the Wainwright estate amid a crush of reporters attempting to stop his vehicle to interview him. She watched his black Porsche Cayenne Turbo S slowly proceed through the crowd of people and equipment, followed by two motorcycle cops. She sneered and popped a lime-flavored corn chip into her mouth. "Fucker," she said to the screen.

When Montgomery reached his residence, he found it crawling with reporters outside and FBI agents inside. He could have been annoyed, but he had knowingly brought this on himself and actually welcomed the intrusion. They would find nothing incriminating in the house, and as soon as they did their search, interviewed all staff members, and confiscated Jody's laptop, they would be gone back to the Wainwright estate, where the action was. He didn't have a personal computer at home; he preferred to do all of his research and communication from his office.

The next morning, promptly at nine, he would be hooked up to a polygraph and would convince the machine that every word he was saying was the gospel truth. And while he was in the presence of a group of law enforcement officials, lying his ass off, the ransom call would come in. That should place him even further down the list of suspects. After all, he couldn't be in two places at the same time.

When the agents had departed, Montgomery retreated to the privacy of his personal bathroom, turned the shower on, and made a call to Bruce. Just to be safe, he was behind two locked doors and the television was on in the bedroom. He was pleased to find his personal geek was almost finished with his project.

He then phoned his less than enthusiastic cohort on *The Quintessence*, who was clearly feeling no pain.

"You might want to take it easy on the booze there, Ramone."

"Or what? You gonna threaten me with death? Too late, so fuck you."

"No, or you're going to run out." He wasn't in the mood for her combative attitude. "How's my wife?"

"Not pregnant. What's that about?"

"Don't know how that leaked out. It was something I threw out at my father-in-law just to rub salt in the wound. So, if you know it isn't true, you and Jody must be talking a lot."

"Actually, we're not."

"That's good. No sense in getting too cozy. She's not going to be around much longer. On the other hand, her impending demise gives you free rein to take whatever you want from her. It's not like she's going to have the opportunity to tell anyone."

"Is there a purpose for this call, other than to make me despise you even more?"

"Just checking in, making sure everything's okay at your end. Tomorrow I'll call you with Bruce's number. I'm going to give you the headlines from the morning Daily Herald and a script of what I want Jody to say. Then you'll call Bruce and have her say *exactly* that. I'll see how that's received and take my cue from there. Who knows? If it looks like they won't pay the ransom, maybe you'll get to kill her tomorrow night, and then you can go on your merry way."

There was a lengthy silence on Tia's end before she finally said, "What about my money?"

"Don't worry about your fucking money, Ramone. You'll get paid, regardless of what happens to Jody."

"Good. Anything else? Because it's lunchtime."

"Nope. Just make sure you're up and sober by seven. That phone call to Bruce is going to be the key to this whole scheme."

"Don't worry about me."

"Of course I worry about you. You'd turn on me in a second if you had the chance." Another dead silence on the other end of the line affirmed the truth of his statement. "Yeah. Just what I thought. That's why I'm not going to let you get the chance."

"If you're finished, I need to go feed your wife."

"Yes, I'm finished. Go have fun with my wife now." He made sure his tone sounded lewd.

"Fuck you."

"You're welcome."

Chapter 15

Dignity is one thing that cannot be preserved in alcohol.
—Anonymous

Tia wanted to throw the phone against a wall and break it into a million pieces. Clearly her passion for hating was as strong as her passion for loving.

The possibility that things might come to a head within twenty-four hours sobered her. She needed to think. There had to be something she could get on the bastard that would take him down. Until then, she needed to continue to sound ruthless, like her normal disagreeable self. She couldn't let on to Montgomery that she would execute him before she would ever harm his wife.

She rummaged in the galley for something she could make Jody for supper, microwaved a Thai chicken dinner and some egg rolls, and put a bottle of iced tea on the tray. Once again, she left the food for Jody to eat alone, politely but firmly refusing to be drawn into a conversation, despite her captive's persistent and charming attempts.

When she returned to retrieve the empty tray, Tia brought along a Sapporo and a split of champagne. If Jody wanted to chat, Tia had some specific subjects she wanted to discuss. Jody was seated on the side of the berth, looking toward the porthole, not paying any attention to Tia's entry. "You okay?" Tia asked.

"Do you really care?" Jody's voice was soft, detached.

"I have to care. You're my responsibility until this is over, so it's up to me to keep you safe. And well."

Jody swiveled to face Tia. This time when their eyes connected, Jody didn't look away. "Are you going to kill me?"

The look of terror in the blue eyes made Tia want to envelop the woman in a tight hug and tell her no, that she was going to try to make everything okay. Tia shifted her weight from one foot to the other. She had to be careful how she answered. Until she actually had devised a plan, she might have to use Jody's fear to her advantage. It might be the only way to save Jody's life. "If everybody does what they're supposed to, you should be fine."

That didn't seem to make Jody feel any better. "And if they don't?"

"Do you honestly think they won't? They know what's at stake."

"Yes. My life."

Tia studied her noncommittally. She stepped toward her and extended the mini champagne bottle, holding up the Sapporo in her other hand. "Join me. I have a few things I'd like to ask you."

Jody stared at the small frosted glass bottle and looked up at Tia. "No, thank you. I'd rather have all my wits together."

"One champagne split gets you drunk?"

"Normally I wouldn't think so, but one glass of wine doesn't get me drunk either. Yet look at the mess that got me into."

"Your wine was drugged." Tia immediately wondered whether she should have revealed that.

"I figured as much, but how? I never left the table."

"Careful planning is how."

"It was the waiter, wasn't it? He's in on it with you."

Tia smiled and offered her the champagne again. "This isn't drugged. The seal hasn't even been broken. Besides, you're already here. What purpose would I have for drugging you?"

Jody shrugged. "I can think of a few things," she said quietly, almost as though she was embarrassed by what she was thinking.

"Trust me, if I was low enough to do *that*, I wouldn't drug you." A wave of heat swept through her at the visual of Jody in her arms under different circumstances.

Jody seemed a little unsettled by Tia's remark but remained silent.

"You wanted me to stay and talk. Come on," Tia said. "Take the split and hold on to it. If you don't want it now, save it for later."

Jody hesitantly took the bottle. "So, what is it you want to ask me?"

"I was watching your family on the news and—"

"How does my father look?" Jody's voice cracked, and she took a deep breath and struggled for composure.

"He actually seems to be holding up well." She had to remember Jody had no access to the news. Tia could tell her anything, and Jody wouldn't know the difference. "I'm more curious about your husband."

"Tony? Why?"

Tia took a long swallow of her Sapporo. "I don't know. You two just don't seem to fit. He seems, well, beneath you."

"Beneath me?" Jody flared. "Shades of my mother," she said toward the ceiling and looked back at Tia. "You don't know him," she said defensively.

Neither do you, Tia thought. "Hey, relax. I'm just sharing an observation." She wanted to ask Jody if she loved her husband, and why. She wanted to know how Jody could have ended up with such a megalomaniac, but she wasn't quite sure how to broach the subject without letting on she was acquainted with the bastard.

"I think you have somehow gotten the wrong impression of him." Jody's fingers nervously played with the foil that encased the cork in the bottle. Tia raised an eyebrow as she took another drink, a patent look of disbelief that prompted Jody to ask, "How can you think that about someone you've never even met?"

"Call it a hunch."

"A hunch? That's rather unfair, don't you think?"

"Perhaps. But my hunches are usually pretty accurate."

"Well, you're not accurate with this one," Jody said finally, not sounding the least bit convincing.

Tia had to know. "Do you love him?"

Jody's eyes flashed up at Tia. "That's none of your business."

"Whether or not you love your husband is none of my business?" Tia was buoyed by Jody's response. "Most women wouldn't have a problem telling anyone and everyone that they loved their husbands, so I guess I got my answer."

Jody seemed flustered as she peeled the foil off the cork and twisted the stopper out of the bottle. The action made a soft popping sound as Tia continued to search her face for any signs of the bitchiness or artifice Tony had attributed to his wife. There didn't seem to be any. Instead, she found Jody almost humble. As the nonplussed heiress took a sip of champagne, Tia smiled.

"You could have chosen any man in the universe. Why would you marry and stay with a man you don't even love?"

"I never said I didn't love him." Jody took a longer swallow, avoiding eye contact with Tia.

"You didn't have to."

"Why are you asking me these questions?"

An amused expression on her face, Tia shrugged. "You wanted to talk. We're talking."

"What possible difference could it make whether or not I love my husband?"

When Jody finally looked directly into Tia's eyes, she lost her breath. Tia wondered why. Was she that frightening? Was it something else? Jody's concentration was focused on the bottle in her tight grasp, and suddenly it was clear to Tia.

She recognized the familiar yielding in Jody's demeanor. *I bet I could seduce you right now.* It didn't matter how Jody might identify her sexuality, she was sending Tia unmistakable signals of attraction. She was probably not even aware she was doing it. *Yep... a little incentive, and I could have her.* But she wanted to make sure that Jody's surrender would be from desire, not fear.

Although sometimes eager to make a conquest, Tia had never crossed that line into rape and didn't intend to start now, especially not with this woman, and not with the amount of alcohol in her own system. If there was ever to be an encounter between them, Tia wanted to recall every detail, unlike those where she couldn't have cared less about anything but getting off.

Tia drained her beer can and held it loosely between her thumb and forefinger as she leaned against the vanity. "It makes no difference. I'm just confused. Honestly, I don't understand the attraction to men, period, but I find it curious that a woman such as yourself would marry a man she didn't love. I'm sure there wasn't a lack of suitors. You're still young, there's a whole world of guys out there. Why this one?"

"You don't understand. Marriage was expected of me."

"And he was convenient?"

"My father thought so."

Tia's brow knit. She wondered why Jody suddenly felt the need to make an admission. "Was your marriage arranged?"

"In a manner of speaking." Jody still didn't look at her.

"There had to be other choices." Why would someone of Jody's social and financial stature have to have a husband picked out for her? And what kind of deal had her father made with the devil to hook her up with Montgomery?

"I'd rather not talk about this," Jody said finally. "What about you? I bet the choices you make about... partners... aren't always perfect."

Cheeky little thing, Tia mused, as memories of the unseemly women she'd had since Colombia sifted through her brain. "People don't usually warm up to me." She anticipated a sarcastic comeback from her captive, expected her to say something like, "Well, what do you expect?"

Instead, Jody took that moment to stare directly into Tia's eyes and in a gentle tone said, "If you don't have fire in yourself, you can't very well warm others, now can you?" This time it was Jody's gaze that was too intense, and it was Tia who had to look away.

If Tia didn't leave the cabin right then, she would be unable to resist approaching Jody, and she would probably do something she would regret. In her inebriated state and hopeful frame of mind, she might have been completely mistaking her odds for a successful seduction, and there was no way she was going to purposely make the ordeal any more traumatic for Jody.

Tia picked up the tray and headed for the door. Surprisingly parched despite the amount she'd been drinking, her question came out in a full rasp. "Anything you need before I lock you in for the night?"

"No," Jody said quietly. "Thank you."

It had been unnerving to be under the scrutiny of the exquisite amber eyes and in the presence of the raw, smoldering sexuality that emanated from every inch of Tia. It took Jody a moment to shake Tia's spell and remember she was a prisoner and still in a dire situation, no matter how attractive or compelling Tia was. Why was she was thinking of her in terms of her being attractive? Tia's dark beauty couldn't be denied, though under the circumstances, those thoughts were dangerously inappropriate. But the honey-colored eyes that bored through her were almost too much to bear. As if being abducted and held for ransom weren't stressful enough.

Jody had seen beyond the impenetrable gaze that had stopped her cold the first time, had seen a spark of life that had initially eluded her. She saw a predatory fire in Tia's eyes, and it sent a shiver down her spine. It gave her a small insight into the many things of which this woman just might be capable. Kidnapping, murder... what else? Rape? Of course that was always a possibility. Just because Tia was a woman made it no less a threat. Jody had already felt Tia's strength, so she had no doubt that Tia was physically able to take her by force. But would she? And why did the idea terrify and excite her at the same time?

Jody was horrified that she was drawn to the thought of Tia overpowering her. She was appalled at her own uncharacteristic lack of judgment and conscience. By all evidence, Tia was not a nice person, and any sexual encounter between them would clearly not be like something out of a lesbian romance novel. Jody was tired and stressed and panicked; she needed sleep and a clear head. She looked at what was left of her champagne split. The last thing she should have done was drink anything that screwed with her perceptions.

Still, she remained totally perplexed by the interaction that had just taken place between her and Tia. She set the small bottle on the nightstand and returned to her berth to lie down. Despite everything, she found Tia fascinating. Even though she fully understood that Tia wasn't her friend but rather someone who could end her life, Jody was drawn to her strength of character, regardless of how jaundiced it might be.

She folded her hands behind her head and stared at the ceiling. Tia's interest in her marriage to Tony puzzled her. Tia had asked some pointed and perceptive questions that seemed to get right to the heart of the sham of her being Mrs. Montgomery. But why? Tia was holding her hostage; shouldn't she have inquired about other things, things pertaining to security and finances?

Tia had stepped into somewhat sacred territory, but Jody's defensive retort had nothing to do with Tia's invasion of privacy. Her reaction to Tia's inquiry and opinion were hasty and well-rehearsed because of her mother. What she really could have told Tia was that it wasn't so much that Tony was beneath her, it was more that Tony wasn't suited to her, and there were several reasons for that, none of which she was going to get into with this stranger.

And yet, Tia didn't feel like a stranger. There was an unusual feeling of kinship Jody experienced toward the ominously feral and oddly magnetic woman. What was she really seeing in those mesmerizing eyes that could one minute appear dull and lifeless, and the next be blazing with intensity? Was it the same fantasy Jody dared not explore? Jody felt heat rising to her face and blamed it on the champagne.

Despite how tired she was, sleep would be elusive without her sleep aid, so she considered how best to put her solitude and wakeful hours to good use. She needed to spend her time concentrating on how to get herself out of this alive instead of being ridiculously engrossed in Tia's simmering sensuality, even if it did divert her mind from a possible imminent death.

Tia was topside, reclining on a deck chair, gazing up at the black, starless sky, a position she had occupied ever since she'd left the master cabin. She had finished another Sapporo and mindlessly held the can, her thoughts clearer than they had been in months.

Tia needed to find something on Montgomery that wasn't connected to this abduction, something that wasn't tied to her, something she could use against him. She wondered if this Bruce guy had any information that might be useful and, if he did, if he would be willing to share. She could speak with him briefly during the next contact call. Should she take the chance that his compliance with Montgomery's demands was as coerced as hers? If so, would he want to jump to a *lighter* dark side and help her save Jody and themselves? She had to know. She would have to take the chance.

That aside, what really drove her crazy was that she wanted Jody. Badly. And, she wanted Jody to want her, too, however unrealistic that might be. What she was feeling was more than lust, it felt deeper, and that not only mystified Tia, it frightened her as well. Her overwhelming longing for Jody Montgomery felt almost... ethereal.

A thought struck Tia like a lightning bolt. Had she been brought to this moment for a reason? She didn't believe in Fate, but if she did, she might have thought she and Jody were destined to meet. That kind of providence was not in Tia's reality. On the off chance that it was true, however, why under these circumstances? And would Jody ever recognize it? And, if so, when? Suddenly, Tia knew that just as surely as Montgomery wanted his wife out of his future, her future was supposed to have Jody in it. For a brief moment, she thought her heart had stopped. It was almost painful to breathe. She cast a glance at the stairway that led to the lower decks.

For the first time in many months, she lost the urge to drink herself unconscious.

Chapter 16

People determine your character by observing what you stand for, fall for, and lie for.
—John L. Mason

Bruce nervously awaited the phone call from the former CIA operative in whose direction he had spinelessly directed his boss. It didn't matter whether she knew he was the one who had gotten her into this predicament; he felt enough guilt for both of them. It didn't matter that he wasn't the one who was going to directly cause Mrs. Montgomery's death; he would be just as culpable as Tia Ramone and Anthony Montgomery.

He checked to make sure all his programs were ready and glanced at his watch. The call should come at any time now.

Montgomery was about to place the call to Tia with the morning headlines. He was sure she would dutifully arrange for Jody's scripted recitation to Bruce, and Bruce would prepare the next call to the Wainwright residence, the one that would demand a ransom and undoubtedly kick off a more intensive search. When he was satisfied that Ramone had the script right, he would go over to the Wainwright estate, where he would be right in the middle of his polygraph when the ransom call came in.

Just a couple more days, and his life would be his own again.

Tia was actually civil to Montgomery when he called. She wasn't sure whether that was due to her waking up without a hangover for the first time in so long that she couldn't even remember the last time, or because the call came in too early for her to have worked up her hostility. She wrote down, verbatim, everything he told her, then went to wake Jody.

She knocked on the door and was surprised when an alert voice told her to come in. She entered and found Jody freshly showered and in a change of clothes that, perhaps intentionally, showed off Jody's physical attributes. Trying not to stare at the obvious, Tia cleared her throat and focused on Jody's face. Jody actually smiled at her. This was an expression she hadn't seen before, and it startled her. A smile? For her? Perfect white teeth were revealed behind rose-colored lips that complemented Jody's lovely, unblemished features, and Tia lost her train of thought for a moment. She recovered and returned her attention to the note in her hand as she approached her.

"No breakfast?" Jody asked. "I'm actually feeling a little peckish this morning."

Tia held out a piece of paper. "We have to do this first." She did her best to sound professional and indifferent, but it took all of her self-discipline to not react to Jody. "You are to say these words exactly as they are written, and it needs to sound as though you're not being forced to say them." The bright expression disappeared from Jody's face as she accepted the paper and silently read the contents of the message.

Tia could guess what Jody was thinking: regardless of any interaction between them, Jody was a prisoner and Tia was her warden. The words Jody was going to repeat no doubt reminded her that Tia was part of a business transaction, one on which her life depended. Tia wished she felt safe enough to tell Jody about Montgomery's involvement.

"Will I be speaking to my father?" Jody's tone was now disheartened.

"No. You actually won't be speaking to anyone, but you need to say it as though you are. I want you to read it over a few times and get comfortable with the words so it doesn't sound like you're reciting it."

Jody glared. "Get comfortable with the words? You think I'm going to be comfortable saying, 'Daddy, you need to pay the ransom or they will kill me'?" She shook her head and folded her arms. "I don't want to say that."

Please don't get rebellious on me now. Tia had to play tough. She stood up straight and her bearing immediately became ominous. Firmly, but only with enough pressure necessary to get Jody's attention, she took Jody's chin between her thumb and forefinger and forced Jody to look at her. "There is no negotiation here. You will say what is written. I don't care how you manage it, just do it. If you don't get it right the first time, we will continue to do it until you do. Got it?"

As Tia removed her hand, Jody bowed her head. *Angry, embarrassed? Maybe both.* Jody appeared to understand that any resistance, no matter how mild, would not be tolerated. Once more, she silently read over what she was expected to say. A sharp nod advised Tia she was ready.

"Let me hear it first." It wasn't a request, and Jody did as she was told. "Okay." Tia displayed her cell phone. "I'm going to make a call. When I hold the phone to your mouth, I want you to say that exactly as you just read it. No short cuts, no embellishments."

Jody bridled at the admonition. "Yes, ma'am."

Tia sighed and shook her head. "Jody, this isn't a game. I have to have your cooperation. I imagine, given a choice, you don't want to say or do anything I ask of you. But if you want to stay alive, you're going to have to do as I tell you."

Cowed, Jody said softly, "I understand."

"Good." Tia searched Jody's face and saw no more insurrection there. Jody's expression reflected a fear that Tia immediately wanted to kiss away. Instead, she stayed on task with the inevitable call. She dialed the number Montgomery had given her, and the connection was made after only one ring. A baritone voice greeted her, and she said, "It's Tia. You ready?"

"Yep. Put her on."

Tia placed the phone to Jody's lips, and Jody began to read. "It's Sunday, September seventeenth. The headline in today's *Herald* is 'Wainwright Heiress Missing, Police Step Up Search,' and right below that is 'Hurricane Lane Leaves Destructive Path in Mexico.' Hi, Daddy. Please don't talk, just listen. I have been abducted. I don't know who my captors are. I'm fine right now and I'm being treated well, but unless you pay them what they ask, I won't be. They've told me they will kill me." Her voice broke. "Please, Daddy, do what they tell you. I love you."

Tia took the phone away and spoke into it. "Get what you need?"

"Got it," Bruce said.

"Great," Tia said flatly and terminated the call. Jody was trying to control her tears by clamping her hand over her mouth, as though that would dam up the flood from her eyes. The stress of it all was obviously getting to her. Tia exercised practiced restraint in not going to her and wrapping her into a comforting hug. "Jody, you know your father will come through." Her tone was as close to consoling as she felt she could be without stepping into compassionate territory.

"I'm sure he'll try," Jody said, getting control of herself. "I don't understand why you'll take a ransom from him and not from me."

"I told you, it isn't about the money."

"What is it about?" Her tone revealed her desperation.

"I can't tell you that." Tia turned and walked toward the door. Jody was upset, but she had also said she was hungry. "I'm going to bring you some breakfast, but only if you're going to eat it."

Jody hesitated, and the hunger won out. "Do we have any bagels?"

"I'll have to look, but I think there are some plain bagels."

"Could I have a toasted bagel with butter, please?"

Jody sounded so shattered, it nearly broke Tia's heart. "Sure."

"Do you cook eggs?"

"Not anything you'd want to eat."

Jody wiped her eyes with the back of her hand and reached for a tissue. "Is there any yogurt?"

"I'll check. Anything else?" Tia turned the door handle.

"Yes. Your coffee sucks."

Tia couldn't help herself; she emitted an uncharacteristic chuckle. The sound of her laughter elicited a strange reaction from Jody. Despite the dire situation she was in, Jody smiled.

Bruce filtered out all background noises from the segment of Jody's call that would be even remotely identifiable and processed his portion of the ransom demand through the computer application. They would be asking one of the richest men in the world for five hundred million dollars in exchange for his daughter's safe return. *Five hundred million dollars.* Montgomery had promised him five million of that. If there was any upside to what he was doing, the payoff would be it. It might even buy off his conscience.

Jody's recitation took fifteen seconds, which gave Bruce forty-four seconds or less for his own script to meet the guidelines Montgomery had provided him. Since he would control the pace of the conversation, it wouldn't be a problem.

When he called the next day with the instructions for how to deliver the money, hopefully Wainwright wouldn't fool around, and by Tuesday this would be over and he would be a millionaire. He tried not to think about his fortune resulting from the murder of an innocent woman. He was afraid that every time he spent some of his blood money, he would remember just how he had "earned" it.

Suddenly he was nauseated. He wished he could find a way out of the plot that wouldn't get him arrested or killed.

The FBI polygrapher was considerably younger than Montgomery had expected him to be. Not that it made any difference. Even an inexperienced examiner trained to read the machine could tell when the instrument was recording deceptive responses.

Fortunately for Montgomery, an old crony had taught him how to beat a polygraph. He hypnotized himself to not believe in the machine's ability to read his mind, which would cause him to not have the sudden nerve jump when he lied. That little trick should, and always had, resulted in his passing the test.

The last time Montgomery had been hooked up to a polygraph, he was being questioned about his ethics and business practices before being awarded a government contract to distribute controlled narcotics. That test was done on an analog machine. Now he was being connected to a digital system—a laptop computer—the needles and scrolling paper replaced by algorithms that would monitor his blood pressure, heart rate, respiratory rate, and electrodermal activity. His hands never did sweat, so the skin response would be the least of his worries. As a practiced liar, he didn't need to put antiperspirant on his fingers or a tack in his shoe to counteract his reactions; he was an expert on duplicity. He had completely fooled his wife, his in-laws, and the staff of his legitimate business for many years, so the typical involuntary, stress-related responses that would tell the examiner his subject was lying were something Montgomery could control, despite the sophistication of the equipment.

His attorney could easily discredit the results of the polygraph; the results of a lie detector test were inadmissible in a court of law. But that wouldn't eliminate him as a suspect in his wife's kidnapping. In order to avoid the FBI's further scrutiny, there was no margin for error in how he came across during this exam.

He took a deep breath and put on his best nervous smile. *Let the games begin.*

As Jed Howard applied the blood pressure cuff and other electronic attachments, he explained the testing procedures, trying to put Montgomery at ease. The forensic psychophysiologist was young, but he was aware that the anxiety brought on by taking a polygraph could cause responses that were interpreted as deception, and how he conducted himself and how he presented the questions could influence the results.

Agent Howard administered a pre-test, asking Montgomery generalized questions about the events that had led to him taking the polygraph. His aim was to get to know Montgomery a little bit. How Montgomery responded would determine how the subsequent questions were designed. When the actual exam started, Howard would ask a dozen or so questions, only four or five of which pertained to the investigation. The rest were control questions, broad inquiries where a lie or truth could easily be detected.

Even though test sessions could sometimes be very boring, Howard needed to remain alert. Not only was he expected to administer the test questions, he was also a trained profiler who analyzed and evaluated the test results. He knew guilty people could pass, and innocent people could fail; it was up to him to put the puzzle together. And, he could be called as an expert witness to testify as to the demeanor of a subject during the testing process.

He took a deep breath and nodded to Mr. Montgomery. *Let the games begin.*

Chapter 17

To know what is right and not do it, is as bad as doing wrong.
—Anonymous

The FBI was listening in as John Wainwright took the phone call from the kidnapper. The billionaire nearly wept when he heard his daughter's frightened voice crack. Sondra Wainwright nearly fainted when she heard the amount of money the abductors were asking. The federal technicians started the trace immediately and stared at their screen in disbelief when the results pinpointed a business district in Shanghai.

"Is that possible?" an agitated Wainwright asked Walt Sanborn after the call had ended and the terms of the ransom demand were dictated. "Could they be holding her in China?"

"Anything is possible," Sanborn said. "They certainly had enough time to get her out of the country. We'll contact our office at the embassy in Shanghai and get them going on this. My gut tells me she's still here, though, still in the U.S., probably still in this state. The abductor's voice sounds almost, well, artificial."

"Artificial? What the hell does that mean?"

"Not real. You weren't talking to a real person. The voice is most likely computer generated." Sanborn could see that Wainwright didn't fully understand the premise. "For example, if you call for train reservations, there's an automated voice that talks to you, interacting with your responses. The vocal inflections are different from those of an actual person. I think that's what we're dealing with here."

"But Jody's voice was real."

"Yes, that was obviously her. I'll talk to my analysts. Her voice could have been prerecorded, although, since she did have the correct headlines from this morning's local paper, if it was prerecorded, it wasn't done that long ago."

Wainwright shook his head. "I don't understand. You think these kidnappers don't exist?"

"Oh, no, Mr. Wainwright, I'm sure they exist. They're just using modern technology to do their dirty work."

"But if she's still here, how could the call come from China?"

"Cleverly. We're obviously dealing with people who have a variety of resources."

"So, in a nutshell, with all of your electronic, digital, and scientific methods, you're no closer to finding my daughter than you were yesterday afternoon, when you had no information at all."

"Mr. Wainwright, we have to dissect the data we just received so that we have a better idea—"

"I don't want you to have an idea. I want you to know. I want my daughter back. Alive!"

"Yes, sir, I understand that but—"

"But nothing. You're advising me not to pay a ransom, and right now, that's the only resolution that I see. I'll call my lawyer and financial advisor and have them start getting the money together."

"Mr. Wainwright, I must strongly advise against that."

John Wainwright put his face close to Walt Sanborn's. "Then find her, goddamn it! Find her before tomorrow's phone call, or you won't be running the show."

Special Agent Sanborn stood and watched the billionaire walk away. He wasn't sure who was turning out to be more difficult to deal with—the emotional Wainwright, or his detached shrew of a wife. At least Montgomery was willing to listen to reason. Sanborn let out a long, exasperated breath, turned and walked back to the command center to talk to his team.

Tia took Jody vanilla yogurt and a toasted bagel. She stayed in the master stateroom only long enough to deliver the tray and returned to the salon to pace and think. The more she saw Jody, the guiltier she felt, so she needed to spend as little time as possible with her. Tia was torn between staying sober and working on a plan to get them out of this mess, or getting rip-roaring drunk and fucking Jody senseless.

She knew she had to call Bruce back, had to find out how deep he was in the plot, and what, if anything, he was willing to do to get out of it. The problem was, if Bruce lacked as many scruples as Montgomery did, she could open a can of worms by trying to enlist his help. He could tip off Montgomery that she was searching for a way out, searching for something, anything, she could get on the bastard to use for bartering.

On the other hand, Montgomery didn't seem the type to share anything equally, including responsibility. She bet that Montgomery had something on Bruce, the details of which could be anything. If he was being threatened by Jody's husband to "do this or else," he might be more than willing to work with her against Montgomery. After all, there was strength in numbers, even if the number was only two. Or Bruce could be a coward and refuse to betray the bastard, thinking he actually would get a reward rather than a bullet. Was she ready to take that chance?

God, she wanted a drink. But she needed a clear head to think things through.

It hadn't taken Jody long to finish her breakfast. The brevity of Tia's appearance left her perplexed. Tia was so hot and cold, mostly the latter, Jody never knew what to expect when Tia entered the room.

When Tia came back for the breakfast dishes, her mood seemed sullen. She didn't look at Jody when she said, "All done?"

"Yes, thank you."

"I'll be back in a few hours with your lunch."

Jody was disappointed when Tia picked up the tray and exited the room without further conversation. Common sense told her she should be grateful for the limited contact, but instead she felt neglected and very, very alone.

The solitude gave her too much time to think about her immediate future, if she had one.

Montgomery went downstairs, secure in the knowledge he had passed his polygraph, not that he ever had a doubt. Wainwright was now in the upstairs study, behind closed doors where the lie detector was set up, being grilled by the forensic psychophysiologist. After him, it was Sondra's turn.

He sought out Agent Marciano to find out what he had missed while he was being tested. The young fed filled him in on the ransom call and what they had determined from it. It didn't bother Montgomery that they had figured out the voice was synthetic, nor did it faze him that they realized the call hadn't originated from Asia. They were no closer to finding his wife. By the time they unraveled the mystery, the ransom would be paid and she and his accomplices would be dead.

Montgomery was being kept abreast of the hunt for his wife. He didn't want the search teams to happen onto *The Quintessence* by accident, so he decided to take that out of the equation.

"Do you think it's at all possible that Jody just got fed up and ran away?" he said to Marciano. "She's been acting unusually antsy the last few weeks. Maybe it was the pregnancy. I've heard women get a little crazy with the sudden hormonal changes, and the responsibility of bringing a Wainwright heir into the world may have been too much pressure for her. She's a lot more mentally fragile than even her parents know."

"Do you think she would set all this up herself just to get lost for a while? No disrespect, sir, but that would be a federal offense."

"Nothing her father couldn't get taken care of. She pleads temporary insanity, agrees to get help. The attorneys on retainer do their legal magic, and it all disappears."

Marciano shook his head in disbelief. "Hypothetically speaking, if she did something like that, any idea where she might go?"

"Well, to start with, has anybody checked the family yachts?"

Chapter 18

Courage is being the only one who knows you're afraid.
—Franklin P. Jones

"Goddamn it! Fucking son of a bitch!" Tia clicked the phone shut. She couldn't believe Montgomery would actually steer the FBI directly to her. She understood the theory behind it, but it didn't make the reality of it any easier. She moved quickly around the deck and the interior of the yacht, picking up any mess she had made, and used the trash compactor to get rid of it. She quickly tidied up the stateroom where she had been sleeping. Satisfied with her hasty cleaning job, she performed a spot-check walk-through and went down to Jody's room.

Tia unlocked the door, opened it wide, and left it in that position. She didn't knock, announce herself, or try to determine where Jody was in the room; she just barged in with a purpose. She headed right toward Jody, who backed up against the wall, startled by Tia's unexpected aggression. Tia grabbed Jody's upper arm and pulled Jody with her as she moved to the head and quickly wiped down any excess water with the bath towel Jody had used that morning. She removed the dirty clothes from the hamper and walked back to the stateroom, Jody in tow.

"What are you doing? What's going on?" Jody was obviously alarmed at Tia's behavior.

Ignoring the question, Tia opened a closet door and placed the laundry items in the very back, behind a stack of shoeboxes. She began to search through drawers. "I need scarves, kerchiefs, anything along that line. Where can I find them?"

"Why?" Fear suddenly bloomed on Jody's face.

"Where?" Tia's grip on Jody's arm tightened, conveying a sense of urgency.

Jody led her to one of the storage containers under her berth. Tia removed the entire drawer. She pulled out several silk scarves, sat Jody down on the bed, and bound her feet together.

"What are you doing?" The quaver in Jody's voice betrayed her panic.

"Just do what I say." Tia finished tying a knot and grabbed for another scarf.

"Please don't do this," Jody begged as Tia tied her hands.

"Shhhh, shhhh, I have to, okay?" Tia was surprised at how soothing her voice was. "No debate here. If you do exactly as I say, you'll be fine. If you don't, I'll have to hurt you."

Jody's eyes grew wide. So far Tia had been benevolent, had treated Jody with as much respect as the situation would allow. However, Tia was quite sure Jody didn't want to test the extent of her temper and her strength.

"Why are you doing this?" Jody's voice trembled.

"My source tells me that this boat is going to be boarded. You can't be found here, and neither can I. This will only be for as long as it takes for them to make sure you aren't here."

After she tied a gag around Jody's mouth, Tia carefully laid her down on the floor and gently pushed her into the bed compartment, face first. Tia slid in behind her and pulled the drawer closed as she inched them in toward the space between the drawers.

The quarters were so close that the women were tight up against one another. Tia knew Jody had to be feeling every curve of her body pressing against her back. She reached over Jody and pushed the opposite drawer out slightly, so she could reposition herself. Tia used the least amount of space possible and pulled that drawer to her, securing them in total darkness, inside the bed.

She didn't want to lie on her right arm for fear it would go to sleep, so Tia maneuvered so it snaked under Jody's neck and around to cup Jody's left shoulder. Her left arm went around Jody's waist to hold them tightly together. Jody had no choice but to rest her head on Tia's bicep, which positioned Tia to breathe into Jody's hair.

They couldn't see each other, but a visual wasn't necessary. Tia was very aware of the full body contact. She could feel Jody take a breath, hear her heartbeat, and sense her apprehension about being that close. She wanted to kiss the back of Jody's head, nuzzle her neck, run her hands over the svelte body.

They had maintained their positions for ten minutes before Tia heard conversation in the distance that indicated someone else was on the yacht.

As the voices and the footsteps got closer, Tia regulated her breathing and gently put her index finger to Jody's top lip. Jody forced herself to draw shallow breaths. Tia started to perspire and wondering whether her thundering heartbeat could be heard outside the compartment. The lack of ventilation and the danger of the moment weren't the only factors that were generating heat.

Danny Marciano and another agent were accompanying Montgomery on the three-yacht tour that started with *The Quintessence*. He was sure they would find nothing relating to the kidnapping, but he was grateful to have something to do away from the estate.

"Why isn't this boat anchored with the other two that are right offshore?" Marciano asked Montgomery as they approached it.

"The only thing I can tell you is that this is where my wife wants it."

Marciano nodded in comprehension. "I guess if it's hers, that's her prerogative."

The FBI agents and Montgomery were aboard a police cruiser that was pulling up alongside *The Quintessence*. "Let me apologize in advance," Montgomery shouted over the noise of the motor and the waves slapping the hull of the boat. "I'm not sure what condition it might be in. Our security guy is usually pretty neat, but I honestly don't remember how he left it."

"Who guards the yacht while he's away?" Marciano asked.

"I promised my wife I would keep an eye on it myself while Kevin's gone. My intention was to get out here once a day, but my schedule at work has been so hectic, I haven't been able to do it. Honestly, unless there have been incidents I'm not aware of, nobody has ever bothered it out here."

"Not a bad gig for a security assignment." Marciano sized up the exterior as the police pilot tied the cruiser to the yacht.

The two agents boarded *The Quintessence* while Montgomery waited on the bridge of the cruiser.

"Aren't you going to walk through with us?" Marciano asked, noticing Montgomery's hesitation.

"If it's all the same to you, I'd rather wait here. If… if God forbid you find something, I'm not sure I can bear to…" Montgomery trailed off.

"It would be helpful if you could accompany us and let us know if anything looks out of place."

"Like I said, not knowing how Kevin left it, I don't know what would be out of place. You guys are the experts. I'm sure if something doesn't look right to you, then it probably isn't."

"As you wish, Mr. Montgomery. We'll be back shortly."

While the other agent looked behind closed doors, Marciano went through the motions of a half-hearted search that included tugging out the drawers under the berths. They were filled with clothes, and he shoved them back in. It took the agents a total of fifteen minutes to search the yacht. They weren't surprised when they didn't find anyone aboard or anything out of place.

"Why are the TV and stereo system from the bedroom sitting out in the living room?" the other agent asked Montgomery once they had joined him back on the bridge of the cruiser.

"Kevin said the room needs to be rewired. He was concerned because the plug kept getting hot, so he just took everything out. I've been meaning to get someone to fix it before Jody has her next party here."

Satisfied with their inspection, the group left to move on to the other two Wainwright yachts.

When Tia pushed at the far drawer with her free arm and foot, she had to stick her lower leg between Jody's knees to get enough leverage. If Jody hadn't felt like she was suffocating, she might have opted to stay where she was for a while longer. Tia had kept to herself, except for those body parts that were, of necessity, pressed against Jody, yet it had been a nearly unmanageable feat of self-control for Jody not to moan.

When the drawer was out, Tia eased Jody forward until her body wormed its way out, Tia right behind her. Tia stood up, reached down, and pulled Jody to her feet. After Tia removed Jody's gag, she ran her thumb over the red scarf mark next to Jody's mouth.

"Are you okay?" Tia asked as she untied Jody's hands and feet.

Jody could only nod. She still reeled from the confinement they had just endured together, being as intimate as they could get without having sex. Tia had held her close for forty-five minutes, had saved her from certain pain by stopping that drawer from being slammed into her, had almost tenderly touched her hair and face. It was too much. Jody's head spun. She sat down on the bed before she could pass out.

Tia placed her hand on Jody's shoulder to steady her. "What's wrong?"

The question was undoubtedly just a formality. Jody was sure Tia knew what was wrong, but she played it out in case she was mistaken. "I don't know," Jody finally answered. "I felt a little dizzy. Probably too much"—she pointed down, toward the vacancy left by the drawer—"of that."

Tia reached into the refrigerator for a bottle of water, twisted off the cap, and handed the bottle to Jody. "Rehydrate."

Feeling quite defenseless, Jody accepted the bottle and looked up at Tia. "Shouldn't you drink something?"

"Oh, I intend to."

Tia peered down into Jody's questioning eyes and revealed the storm raging in her own. Jody wanted Tia to reach down and caress her face like she had before. Instead, she saw Tia ball up her fist and keep it at her side, as though to redirect the energy of the licentious tempest that appeared to be brewing within them both. Her expression undoubtedly telling Tia the feeling was mutual, Jody felt emotionally exposed.

The electrified air between them jolted Jody to her core. Seconds seemed like hours as neither of them broke eye contact. The continuous current that looped through Jody damned near made her blood boil. She had never experienced anything quite like it.

What the hell is happening? Jody felt the fluttering feeling she only got when she was sexually excited. She briefly closed her eyes and tried to will it away. It had to be fear. Or fatigue. *Please, God, let it be fear or fatigue.*

Jody shot a glance at Tia, unable to avoid the hot, tawny gaze that had stirred her before and continued to have a profound effect. Tia's impossibly sultry expression, once again, left Jody breathless.

"I'll bring back some lunch for you," Tia said, moving toward the door.

Jody was positive it was her unmistakable reaction to Tia that was prompting Tia to cut their interaction short. "I'm... I'm too upset to eat," Jody said.

"Then I'll be back at suppertime with something for you."

"Okay." She watched Tia's back as she walked to the door. "Tia?"

Tia turned toward Jody's voice but didn't look at her. "Yes?"

"Thank you."

"For what?"

"Stopping that drawer from hurting me when he kicked it back in."

Tia nodded. "I told you, I need to keep you safe and well until this is over."

"I think it's more than that. I think that deep down inside, you're a decent person."

"You're wrong. Anything else?"

"I'm not wrong," Jody said quietly.

Tia closed the door behind her and locked it.

Jody perched on her berth in stunned disbelief. She took a long drink of the cold water, which did nothing to cool her flushed body. She pondered the spot she was in. To say her life was a mess would be a gross understatement. On top of everything else, she could no longer deny her unmistakable sexual attraction to the woman who held her hostage. She had clearly been aroused by the woman who might very well kill her.

Indisputably, Tia was stunning and innately sensual, and she had an unquestionably commanding presence, but to feel such an unexpected... desire... for her... Maybe she could blame it on the power of the suggestive eyes that disclosed Tia's own libidinous inclinations.

No. That would be a lie. It was time to stop kidding herself. She had to acknowledge her own carnal longings for what they were. *Okay, fine! You're attracted to women. You admitted it. Happy now? Get over yourself.*

The problem was, it wasn't herself she needed to get over. She was turned on by the woman who held her life in her hands, and the more time she spent with Tia, the more difficult it was to hide her feelings. Jody pounded her fists on the bed. When had she lost her mind? She couldn't let Tia know the erotic sensations that surged through her at the sight of her exotic beauty. The whole scenario was just wrong. If she got out of this alive, her shrink certainly would be earning his money during their next session.

Jody retreated to the head to take another shower. More cold water than hot this time.

Chapter 19

Choice, not chance, determines destiny.
—Jean Nidetch

Tia tried to keep a clear head, tried not to act on the personal feelings she had developed toward her captive, tried to stay away from the booze, but it was all too much. She wasn't that strong yet. After she showered the sweat from her overheated body, she drank heavily the rest of the day.

The beguiling heiress wasn't the pretentious bitch Montgomery had made her out to be. On the contrary, she appeared to be one of the nicest, most down-to-earth women Tia had ever met. Tia was quickly reaching a point where she wouldn't be able to play her part any longer.

Jody was petrified; that was obvious, regardless of how she tried to disguise it. Tia was besieged with an acute attack of conscience. She didn't just need a new deal; she needed a whole new deck of cards. She poured herself another shot of the good stuff and chased it down with the rest of her beer.

She placed the scotch bottle on a small table and settled into a seat on the bridge that faced the vast expanse of the ocean. When the cell phone rang, she clenched her teeth and drew in a deep breath. She really did hate Montgomery. As she reached back into the refrigerator for a cold beer, she flipped open the burn phone.

"Yeah?"

"Nice job, Ramone. If they suspected anything, they hid it well. I think you're safe there until we conclude this little operation." Montgomery sounded very pleased with himself.

"Define safe," she growled. She opened her beer and took a long swig.

"Are you always this surly?" His voice conveyed amusement. "I would think that after being in such close physical proximity to my wife, you would be thanking me."

"If you think your wife is so fucking hot, why the hell do you want her dead?"

"She is a delectable little morsel, but I can get that anywhere."

"And you think I can't? I've got news for you—"

"Yeah, whatever. I'm not wasting time arguing about whose is bigger. So how is the little woman after her ordeal this afternoon?"

She was tired of his arrogance and smugness. "You'll be happy to know that she was all over me. Your wish finally came true." There was dead silence on the other end of the line, which made Tia smile. "What's the matter, Montgomery? Cat got your tongue? I thought you'd be happy to know a certain pussy had mine, too."

"You're kidding me," he said finally, his tone one of disbelief. "You are kidding me, right?"

"I thought this was what you wanted, what you fantasized about. Yeah, she's quite the hot little ticket. Very responsive. I guess being so close to me in that tiny compartment triggered something in her. I have to tell you, Montgomery, she's very, very eager to please. Why you'd want to get rid of that, I don't know."

His voice sounded strangled. "You're telling me that you fucked my wife?"

"No. She fucked me, and she left me wanting. I'm sure tonight when I go back for more—"

He snorted. "Now I know you're bullshitting me. You can't be talking about my wife. Beautiful, yes; phenomenal body, yes; but she's more than a little boring in bed."

"Maybe in your bed." Tia reveled in the lack of an immediate retort from Montgomery.

Finally he said tightly, "Did you rape my wife, Ramone?"

"You can't rape the willing. Besides, why are you sounding pissed? Like I said, I thought this was what you wanted."

Just as she had suspected, his fantasy was better than the reality. Tia was sure the actual thought of her having sex with his wife wasn't anywhere near as stimulating as Montgomery had assumed it would be, for no other reason than that until Jody was dead, she was still his property. All dirty jokes aside, he was a very possessive man.

But she didn't want him to think that, because of this imagined intimacy, Tia would be less likely to kill his wife. That might make him change his plans. She needed time to think about how to get herself and her captive out alive and, hopefully, unharmed. Now that she'd had her fun, it was in her best interests to placate him.

Tia laughed. "You're such an idiot, you know that, Montgomery? I haven't touched your wife. She's terrified, and I'm keeping her that way. But thanks for letting me know you couldn't satisfy her in bed."

"I never said that." His tone bordered on being defensive. "Even if she did go for women—which she doesn't, so I know the only way you'd get her would be by force—she's too damned inhibited to be satisfied in bed."

"No woman is inhibited if she has the right partner."

His conceit returned. "Trust me, if I couldn't open her up, nobody could."

Tia rolled her eyes and made a gesture like a male jerking off. "I'm sure. So what's on the agenda for tomorrow?"

It turned chilly after the sun disappeared. Tia looked out at the view and stood up from the deck chair. She hooked the scotch bottle and descended the staircase to the salon. She placed the bottle back in the cupboard and contemplated her next move very carefully. Her nonstop intake of alcohol, her recollection of the day's events, and her conversation with Montgomery about his wife had worked her up to frenzied horniness. If it had involved any other woman, Tia would have accepted the unspoken challenge that Montgomery presented regarding his wife's restraint in bed. But she couldn't look at Jody as a conquest, or as a pawn in Montgomery's sick game.

All the same, Tia decided she had to have Jody; she could no longer withstand that magnetic pull. She was pretty sure Jody wanted her, too, except she wasn't sure Jody had recognized it as sexual desire. Or maybe she had. The candidly wanton look in Jody's eyes spoke volumes, as did her distracted, flustered behavior that afternoon after being enclosed in the compartment together, and even the night before, when she said to Tia, *"If you don't have fire in yourself, you can't very well warm others, now can you?"* At least it spoke volumes to the desperately lonely Tia Ramone.

Tia quietly unlocked the master stateroom door and closed it behind her. She let her eyes adjust to the dark and studied Jody's still form, supine on the covers. Jody Montgomery was so beautiful, so vulnerable, so trusting in slumber. Tia knew Jody was exhausted, knew she fought losing consciousness for fear of it being her last sleep. The first day, Tia mightn't have cared, but now, a little less than forty-eight hours since she had taken her hostage, Tia knew she wouldn't, couldn't hurt her, at least not in a violent way. Something about Jody Montgomery drew her in, was almost familiar, and Tia was overwhelmed by the need to sexually connect with her.

Tia settled on the bed as lightly as possible so she wouldn't startle Jody into wakefulness. She stretched out behind the sleeping form and slowly snuggled in close, up against her. Almost instantly, Jody, still asleep, cuddled back into Tia's body, as though it were routine. Tia gingerly placed her hand on Jody's hip, lightly traced a pattern from hip to shoulder, and repeated the movement several times. Tia tilted her head down to nuzzle the side of Jody's face and inhaled the fragrance of her fruit-scented shampoo. She buried her nose in the short, blonde mane and began kissing Jody's neck, from her earlobe to her collarbone. That's when she felt the smaller woman stir.

Jody moaned lightly in her sleep, and Tia's hand snaked around the trim waist and drew their bodies closer together. Tia nipped lightly at the inviting, delicate throat and followed with slow kisses. Her hand slipped under Jody's blouse and connected with warm skin. Tia felt the involuntary shiver and stroked up Jody's ribcage to make lazy circles around Jody's breast. Tia smiled as her thumb brushed over a very stiff nipple. She cupped Jody's full breast and lightly pinched the erect tip, eliciting another moan from deep within Jody's chest.

Tia propped herself up on her right side to give herself better access, and her lips left a trail of kisses along Jody's cheekbone. She touched Jody's mouth with her own, and unexpectedly, Jody turned her face toward Tia, seeming to seek more direct contact. Tia was amazed to find Jody was still out of it, that the reaction appeared unconscious.

Jody's lips were very soft, very kissable. A thrill surged through Tia as she pressed her mouth to Jody's. Jody responded so strongly, Tia had to pull her head back to see if Jody's eyes were open. She was surprised to see that Jody was still, for the most part, asleep.

She continued to lovingly assail Jody's mouth as her hand pursued a manipulation of Jody's breasts. Suddenly she felt Jody's fingers on her face. They caressed her chiseled cheekbone before finding their way to the back of her head and tangling in her hair. Jody's other hand covered Tia's and her lips parted.

As Tia dueled with Jody's challengingly gratifying tongue, she realized that Jody had awakened, albeit slowly. She slid her fingers down the front of Jody's cotton panties and felt wetness soaking the material. Her hand slipped inside the undergarment and massaged the moist, soft curls. It pleased her when Jody arched into her touch with a loud moan. Tia slithered two fingers over the well-lubricated area, circled and teased Jody's clit, applying a little more pressure each time. The longer the strokes, the more intense the contact, the harder Jody breathed.

Now wide awake, Jody couldn't have pushed Tia away even if she'd had the presence of mind. What Tia was doing felt so good, so needed, so wanted. Her mild bucking encouraged Tia to continue stroking, and Jody felt a whirlpool of emotions swirling within her, a sensation between her legs she hadn't felt since... ever. So fast and so strong did her climax build and pump through her, she thought she would burst.

Tia stopped kissing Jody and studied her as she teetered on the edge. Their eyes locked. Tia's gaze was ferocious, expectant, while Jody's showed desire, surprise, and gratitude, but no apprehension.

Jody closed her blue eyes, now darkened by a hunger she never knew existed within her. She tilted her head back and opened her mouth to scream her release. Instead, she buried her face in Tia's shoulder and muffled her cries against Tia's jersey, quivering as the orgasm continued to roll through her.

"Come on," Tia whispered into her hair, "let it out. Nobody's going to hear you but me. Let it out."

The impossibly sultry voice and the fact that Tia never stopped stroking her almost instantly brought Jody to a second orgasm. She dug her fingers into Tia's arms and prepared for the sensation to wash over her. Only this time, when the climax hit her, she did as Tia urged, and yelled her release with "Oh God," "Oh fuck," and "Tia," before she regained control of her senses and her body.

Tia held Jody as she relaxed back onto the bed in the same position she had been before they started. Tia felt Jody shudder, and she rose to one elbow and discovered that Jody was weeping quietly.

"Jody... please don't cry," Tia whispered in her ear.

Jody moved from Tia's embrace, curled up into a fetal position, and folded her arms protectively across her body. "I can't believe I just let you do that." Her hushed voice was laced with shame.

Tia brushed her lips over Jody's ear and lightly outlined the delicate shell with the tip of her tongue. She felt Jody stiffen, but was unable to discern whether it was from regret and horror or from resisting her own traitorous urges. "It's okay—"

"No. It is *not* okay. Jesus! What is this? Do I have a sign on me that says 'fuck me while I'm sleeping'? Please go. Please, Tia."

Embarrassment and anger burning in her, Tia was suddenly sober and momentarily frozen in place. Had she been wrong? Had she just forced herself on someone unable to resist her because of intimidation? *No, no, no.* She wouldn't be able to live with herself if fear had been the cause of Jody's submission. She didn't want to leave the cabin without an explanation for Jody's sudden retreat.

Tia rolled Jody over and straddled her. She grabbed Jody's wrists and pinned them to the bed, making Jody focus on her. At first Jody looked afraid and exposed, but then she got angry and tried to fight her way free of Tia's grasp, only there was no way she could match the stronger woman's energy and muscle. "Get off me, Tia. Let me go."

"Not until you answer a few questions," Tia said evenly, her eyes narrowed. Tia might be wrong about many things, but she never misread the signals of attraction. She had almost a sixth sense about when even the most aloof woman wanted her. She wished Jody would stop struggling. Her movements were firing up Tia's libido in the worst way. "Why are you so pissed off? You certainly didn't act like what I was doing was against your will. If you had told me to stop, I would have."

Jody scuffled to achieve her physical freedom, but Tia had to exert only a little effort to hold her down, and finally Jody surrendered and stopped wrestling with her. Jody's tears began again. "I don't want to have these feelings for you," she finally said. She breathed the words out as though she had been fighting to keep air in her lungs and had to exhale.

"Why?"

"Why?" Jody looked as if she was about to laugh at the question, but apparently she realized Tia was deadly serious. "You abducted me. You're holding me hostage, and you're probably going to kill me once you get the money." The impact of her own words seemed to suddenly strike her like a hard slap in the face, and her eyes promptly stung with renewed tears.

Tia felt the need to immediately comfort and reassure her. She knew she had to tell Jody she would never kill her, would never allow one hair on her head to be harmed. "Shhhh, shhhhh, Jody, no. No." Tia loosened her grip on Jody's wrists. "Listen to me.

Shhhhh." When she had Jody's undivided attention, she continued. "I'm not going to kill you. I give you my word."

Jody's expression showed her incredulity. "Your word? Jesus Christ, Tia."

"Okay, all right. I know that sounds ridiculous under the circumstances, but—" Tia thought about what she was saying; of course it made no sense. She hadn't exactly exhibited that she had Jody's interests at heart—holding her captive in a secluded, self-contained area until she got paid handsomely for the task. She relaxed her grip on Jody's wrists as her anger dissipated. "Jody, I don't want to hurt you. Not any more than I already have."

"Then why are you doing this?" The words emerged as a hiss, but there was a genuine question in her eyes.

"Because your husband is paying me to." It slipped out before she thought about it. Startled by her own indiscretion, Tia wondered if it was Freudian, intentional. Her surprise at herself was no match for the stunned look of ultimate betrayal and hurt on Jody's face.

"Wh-what? No. Not Tony. No. I know things aren't perfect between us and that he has a greedy side, but… no. Tony has it too good to do something like this. Why did you say that? It's a lie!"

"I'm sorry, but the truth is that your husband is behind all of this." Tia released her grasp but remained astride Jody's hips. She waited for her words to be absorbed.

Jody became more agitated. "You're lying! Why would he? He has everything. Why would he risk it all by doing this?"

"I don't know the answer to that. I guess he wants out of the marriage and doesn't want to settle for what he'd get from a prenup. Why would I lie to you?"

"Why wouldn't you lie to me?"

"How do you think I got access to this yacht? Why do you think your personal security officer was so conveniently sent on vacation right now? How do you think I had the inside scoop that we were about to get boarded? How do you think I knew about that space under the bed? Your husband set all this up. He's protecting me… at least until your family pays the ransom. What happens after that is anybody's guess. For both of us."

What Tia said started to sink in, and Jody's hurt and confusion at the thought of her husband's betrayal burst from her lips. "I don't believe you!" But she must have, and that was what undoubtedly fueled her angry outburst. She furiously punched at Tia as her outrage exploded.

Flying fists battered against Tia's shoulders, one blow actually connecting with the side of her face. When she was finally able to get control of Jody's wrists, Tia held them to the bed, one on either side of Jody's head. Jody struggled, almost bucking Tia off her, which prompted Tia to reposition herself so she could immobilize Jody. "Stop! Stop it. I am not going to hurt you."

The look in Jody's eyes was belligerent yet wounded. Tia could only imagine that Jody was feeling the sting of the ultimate betrayal, but their thrashing about was triggering rabid lust in Tia and she couldn't resist the temptation. She stretched out on top of Jody, lowered her face, and seized Jody's mouth with her own. It was a bold, arrogant move to try to change Jody's rage into passion.

Jody stubbornly tried not to react to Tia's lips. Their movements were sparking more than longing within her. Becoming aroused by being held down by Tia, Jody finally ceased struggling and began to return the kiss with equal fervor. Heat rising between her thighs, Jody wrapped her legs around Tia's waist. Rotating her hips and pushing her pubic bone against Tia's belly elicited a growl. In one swift, fluid motion, Tia extricated herself and almost ripped Jody's beach pants off her. This aggression only served to fuel Jody's desire, and she watched in helpless fascination as Tia quickly stripped her of all clothing.

As Tia slowly scanned Jody's body, Jody found it difficult to breathe. No one had ever looked at her like that before, with such fiercely untamed wanting, yet an almost gentle adoration and appreciation that paralyzed her with a deep-seated need, a need such as she had never felt. Jody's hands found the front of Tia's jeans and grabbed on, pulling the stronger woman down to her. Tia settled her body over Jody's, completely covering her, and Jody stared up into impatient amber eyes that held an expression that displayed vulnerability and an unsated hunger, a combination that Jody found intoxicatingly irresistible.

"Jody..." Tia's voice was hoarse with desire, and Jody wondered if Tia could have elevated it above a whisper if she tried. "I have to have you. All of you. It would be very hard to stop, but I will if you tell me to."

"I know it's wrong, but I want you, too. I—" Quieted with a smoldering kiss, Jody closed her eyes and allowed herself to bask in the sheer bliss of the moment. She had never been kissed the way Tia was kissing her. Nothing had ever elicited the sexual frisson that surged through her now. She was awed by the way her body responded, rapt with the sudden knowledge that this was what it was supposed to feel like when someone made love to her.

As Tia brushed her lips against every area of Jody's body, Jody savored each sensation, wishing each touch would last forever. Sometime between Tia resting on top of Jody or hovering above the red-blonde curls that covered her mound, Tia had discarded all of her own clothes. Jody cursed herself for not paying attention, as this was a body she really wanted to see up close and personal, but Tia had kept her deliciously occupied.

"Tia. Tia." Jody was breathless at the thought of what Tia was about to do to her, but she needed to get her attention.

"Yes?" Eyes the color of dark gold looked up and locked with Jody's.

"Don't hold back."

Tia's look of desire was so overpowering, Jody recognized that Tia wouldn't be restrained, would indeed fuck her hard and completely, and wouldn't be at all concerned with whether or not it was something Jody was used to.

She acknowledged Jody's wishes with a slight nod, her smile feral as she returned to nuzzling the damp curls. Tia kissed Jody's center before she parted her nether lips and firmly assaulted her with her tongue. Jody's hand in Tia's hair pushing her head closer and the gyration of Jody's hips were meant to tell Tia she was right on target in her appraisal of what Jody wanted. Jody had no doubt Tia would show her a side of sex she had never known.

Evening became night and night became morning. At some point before the sun rose, they fell asleep, so tangled up in each other that it was difficult to decipher where one body ended and the other started.

Chapter 20

Ability is rated by what is finished, not what is attempted.
—Anonymous

At first light, Jody quietly slipped out of bed and threw on her robe. She stood at the side of the berth and observed the long, naked body of the woman who, just hours before, had done magical things to her. She also thought of the things that she had done, things that she would never have dreamed she had the ability to give. Her body still tingled with the residual passion thrumming through her. She studied the gorgeous, sensuous woman, and visions of their raw fucking rippled within her. Her arousal began to build again, and she knew if she didn't get out of that room, she wouldn't be able to keep herself from attacking Tia. She was sure such an advance wouldn't be met with any resistance, but she needed to let her body rest from the force with which she had been taken and the aggression with which she had responded. That Tia was dangerous only enhanced Jody's excitement, as did the sexual play that was different, more fulfilling. She unabashedly craved more.

But Jody was still a captive, and regardless of the sudden, overwhelming change in her relationship with Tia, she didn't know whether she could trust the intriguing woman. With that little bit of suspicion still at the forefront, Jody sidled over to the door and kept her eyes on Tia while she tried the handle. When the door opened freely, Jody remembered that Tia had removed the interior lock and couldn't have secured the door from the inside.

Jody quietly shut the door behind her, pushed the bolt closed, and rested her forehead against the cool surface of the frame. If Tia was lying to her, this was her chance to escape. If Tia was telling her the truth, and Tony was behind the kidnapping, escaping might put her in even greater danger. If Tia had lied just to get Jody to have sex with her, she would have left the room afterwards and locked her back in. If Tia told the truth just to clear her conscience for wanting to have sex with her, Tia could still be her only hope of getting out of the situation without further harm. Jody closed her eyes and opened the bolt with a sigh. She was amazed that she would rather take her chances with an unpredictably contentious, unmistakably amorous kidnapper than the man to whom she had been married for over three years, a man she obviously didn't really know at all.

In the salon, Jody stopped to contemplate her next move. She had a lot to consider, but she determined the very first thing she wanted was a decent cup of coffee. Maybe Tia was exceptional at everything else she put her mind to, but she couldn't make coffee for shit. Jody walked into the galley and activated her Jura Capresso Impressa F9. She figured that the only reason Tia's coffee was so bad was that she probably didn't have the patience to figure out such a high-tech machine. How many coffeemakers had a touch screen with Internet connectivity? How many coffeemakers cost nearly two thousand dollars? Her perfect cup of brew in hand, she climbed the stairs to the deck to watch the full sunrise and consider her options.

Tia drifted slowly into consciousness. With a sigh of contentment, she stretched her muscles against the effects of the marathon sex. The enthusiasm with which Jody had readily and vigorously participated was surprising from someone who had never been with a woman. Tia had expected a reserved, strait-laced neophyte, not the forward, wild, no-holds-barred woman who eagerly satisfied her every desire. Before they had fallen asleep, Jody remarked with wonder that she didn't know what had gotten into her, a statement that made Tia bubble with laughter, for which she received a spirited swat on the ass.

Jody had held Tia tightly to her and told her she had no idea her body was capable of feeling such pleasure. Obviously, Tia had awakened something dormant in Jody, unleashed something primal within her, and she hoped there was no reining it back in.

Tia suddenly realized the other side of the bed was empty. Panic rose in her throat, nearly strangling her. She flew off the berth, taking only three steps to reach the door, expecting it to be bolted from the outside. In her selfish urgency to have sex with Jody the evening before, she hadn't thought about the fact that she couldn't secure the door from the inside after she entered the stateroom. She felt she had convinced Jody that she wasn't going to hurt her, and they would figure out an escape together, but still, she had abducted Jody and held her for ransom. With Tia confined, Jody could drive the yacht right up to the marina and have the cops waiting to arrest her.

Tia took a deep breath and wrapped her fingers around the door handle. When she tentatively pushed down on it, the door easily opened outward. Relieved, she stood there until her eyes adjusted to the brilliant sunlight, then she searched the salon and the galley for her new lover. Jody could also have easily taken the dinghy back to shore, and Tia's panic threatened again, until she smelled the inviting aroma of freshly brewed coffee.

Jody descended the stairs from the bridge, mug in hand. Blue eyes captured tawny ones, and a smile of almost shy contentment greeted Tia, who leaned against the door.

"Happy to see me, I see," Jody teased, giving Tia an overt once-over.

Tia glanced down at her taut nipples and grinned. "In more ways than one."

"Did you think I had left to turn you in?"

"It crossed my mind."

"Why don't you get dressed and join me for a cup of coffee, and we can talk about it?"

"Does my nudity bother you?"

Jody grinned. "Bother me? No. But it is distracting, and I really think we should talk about our situation. You sit near me in that state, and I can't guarantee we'll get any talking done."

Tia smirked. "And that would be bad because…?"

Jody laughed as she pointed. "Go put some clothes on."

Before Tia retreated inside the master stateroom, she and Jody exchanged a heated look. Tia had no doubt she and the sexually adventurous heiress would warm the sheets again long before the sun went down. She knew that the flash fire between her legs could only be extinguished by one woman. Anticipating their next encounter, she dressed quickly and joined Jody in the galley.

She had chosen to wear a sleeveless T-shirt and a pair of Tony's boxer shorts she found in the drawer under the bed. Her tanned and toned arms and legs were a clear contrast to the pale, exposed limbs of the fairer woman seated opposite her. Tia took a sip of the steaming beverage and smiled. "I should have let you out sooner to make the coffee."

"So, you don't really like it awful, you just couldn't be bothered to crack the code of the complicated coffee machine," Jody said, teasing.

"I was afraid I'd break it, so I just made instant."

"Oh. Well, that explains why your coffee sucked out loud. All you have to do is push the button, and it makes coffee that rivals Starbucks."

"I'd rather have Dunkin' Donuts." Tia took another sip as she looked out over the water, then she focused on her new lover. "Why didn't you run?"

Under the scrutiny of intent dark golden eyes, Jody didn't look away. She leaned forward and rested her elbows on her knees. "I thought about it. I really did. For about a minute. I even locked the door. And then I unlocked it. I realized I believed you. I believed you, basically a total stranger, believed that my husband is behind this, without even talking to him about it. How pathetic is that?" Jody looked as though she was on the verge of tears, torn between disgust and sadness.

Tia leaned forward and took Jody's hands in her own. "Is that the only reason you didn't run?"

"No." Jody's voice was scarcely above a whisper. "I don't want to believe you're a bad person." She looked down at their joined hands. "I don't want to think you've come into my life just to do me harm."

"Originally, that's exactly why I was here. But now? I couldn't hurt you, no matter what." She lifted Jody's fingers to her lips and kissed them.

"I believe you, Tia. I know I shouldn't, but I do. If I wasn't listening to my gut instinct, you'd be in custody right now." Jody looked surprised at the boldness of her own statement. "Does Tony just want money, or does he want me dead?" Tia's reluctance to respond gave Jody her answer, and Tia watched helplessly as Jody broke down. "First, my abduction, and then finding out my husband is behind it, and he doesn't just want money, he wants me dead."

Tia pulled Jody into a tight embrace and positioned her on her lap. "Listen to me," Tia said firmly. "I don't know what kind of marriage you two had, but he's an idiot to want you out of his life, by whatever means. I'm very much hoping that his loss will be my gain."

"We don't even know each other. I know nothing about you, and all you think you know about me probably comes from what you've read in the papers. Granted, we just spent an incredible night together, but you have to admit, Tia, it was under the most extraordinary of circumstances. I don't know you. You could still be playing me."

"I could, but I'm not. I want to get to know you better. A lot better." Tia cuddled Jody closer and wiped away her tears. "I don't give a flying fuck about your wealth. I don't care that you're high profile or that your family is famous. Your bank account doesn't impress me. I want that out in the open right away. My last lover was extremely well-off, but it wasn't the reason I was with her."

"Did you abduct and take advantage of her, too?" Jody sniffed and ran her finger lightly along the pattern embroidered on Tia's T-shirt.

Tia could feel the smile on Jody's face against her shoulder, and Jody's tone seemed congenial enough. "No."

"You like to pick up rich women?" Jody tucked her head into the curve of Tia's neck, and Tia responded by putting her arms around Jody and clasping her hands together over a curvy hip.

"It's the woman, not the money that I'm interested in."

"You do realize this is insane," Jody said.

"I couldn't agree with you more. My life is insane. I've needed the insanity to stop for a while now, but nothing has even come close to giving me the incentive to turn my life around, to be the responsible person I once was. Until you."

"Why me?" Jody's tone was intrigued… and hopeful.

Tia shrugged as much as her shoulder would allow with a blonde head lying against it. "Other than you being beautiful and, seemingly, a decent person, I honestly don't know."

"How much was Tony going to pay you to finish me off?"

Tia expelled a long breath and her shoulders slumped. "Ten million dollars."

"That's all? Huh. Nice to know what my husband thinks I'm worth."

"Actually… he's asking your dad for five hundred million."

Jody bolted up and looked directly at Tia. "And you're only getting ten? Oh dear, you need a business manager."

"Honestly, I cared less about the amount of money than I did about having enough to get me out of the States and started elsewhere. I would have probably pissed it all away on women and booze anyway."

"Well, that's a glowing attempt to persuade me to be with you."

It surprised Tia that Jody was being so playful when they were talking about the going rate for killing her.

"So what changed your mind about doing it?" Jody asked.

"You did." Tia kissed the top of Jody's head. "When I got dragged into this, I honestly had no idea I was supposed to kill you. I thought I was supposed to keep you here, out of sight, until the ransom was paid. After I got you here, your husband changed the plan."

"Would you actually have done it?"

"If you're asking me if I'm capable of killing, the answer is yes. If you're asking me if I wanted to do it, the answer is no."

Jody sighed and slid her arm around Tia's waist. "It's wrong, my wanting to be with you, isn't it?"

"I don't know if it's wrong, but I can assure you it's probably not wise."

"Are you purposely trying to dissuade me from succumbing to your not-so-subtle charms?" Jody said, patting Tia's belly.

"You mean it isn't already too late?" Tia teased back. "I'm just saying we need to have a little chat about my past before you make any decisions about me."

"Should we talk about that before we discuss what we're going to do about my abduction and impending demise?"

"I think we should." Tia wanted a drink. Certain that someone as cultured and dignified as Jody would be horrified and repelled by her history, Tia wanted to start herself on her daily path to numbness before she revealed all. Maybe Jody would surprise her. After all, Tia had already been pleasantly surprised to find that Jody wasn't at all refined in bed. The thought elicited a lascivious smile and a bolt of unexpected heat between her legs.

She bit back the urge to deposit Jody on a chair and grab a beer and the bottle of scotch. The tightening of Jody's arms encouraged Tia to stay where she was. She reassuringly kissed Jody's neck.

This sent a visible shiver through Jody, and she tilted her head back to look at Tia. "You keep doing that, and we're never going to get anywhere except right back in bed."

"Again, that would be bad because...?" Tia's voice was husky.

Eager eyes engaged Tia's. "We'll never get anything else accomplished. And as much as I really want you to fuck me senseless again—and oh, God, do I—I think this discussion is just the slightest bit more important."

The expression Jody wore was so unintentionally coy and inviting, it was hard for Tia to tear her eyes away. "Unfortunately, you're right." She lifted Jody's chin and kissed her one more time before their dreaded talk.

They made out longer than either had intended; it had been difficult to stop kissing and move apart.

Jody couldn't fathom her body's impulses, the magnetic tug that fueled her desire to touch this beautiful, yet dangerous woman. She couldn't recall ever being so drawn to anyone in her life. Every time she even glanced at Tia, she was immediately aroused. Finally she took the initiative to push herself away and take a seat back in her own chair. "Okay, what is it you think I need to know?"

"Everything." Tia folded her hands on the table and rested her forehead on her knuckles. She took a deep breath, sat up, and looked beyond Jody, out to sea. "One thing you need to know is that I'm a drunk." She winced. Her expression blank, Tia focused on her companion. When Jody didn't comment, Tia continued. "It's because I'm a drunk that I got into this mess. But let me tell you a little bit about my past..."

Chapter 21

When I let go of what I am, I become what I might be.
—Lao Tzu

"You were CIA?" Jody was wide-eyed.

"I know. Hard to believe, right?"

"Yes. No. I don't know. I guess not. I mean, what happened? Why are you ex-CIA?" Jody asked. *The CIA? Could this get any more convoluted?*

"I was accused of betraying my country, so I was burned."

Jody blanched and leaned forward. "Did you... betray?" Her voice was a whisper.

"No. My country betrayed me. Or at least The Agency did," Tia said quietly. "I was a good operative, Jody. I was dedicated. I knew nothing else but the CIA. That's how much I loved my job. My life was my work. Literally." Tia really looked like she could use a drink. Perhaps many of them.

"What went wrong?"

"I followed orders," Tia told her, "which was ultimately my downfall. That assignment should have been my ticket to the top. It should have won me a Distinguished Intelligence Medal."

"A what?"

"It's a coveted award for an achievement of a distinctly exceptional nature."

"Sounds important." Should she believe what Tia was about to tell her? After all, she had no way to confirm Tia's story. She needed to hear more before she made a decision. "Please, go on."

"I was deep into an assignment monitoring Euskadi Ta Askatasuna." At Jody's blank look, she added, "They're a group fighting Spain for an independent Basque state. Anyhow, I was suddenly yanked from that and briefed for an existing assignment another operative was handling. Because I was an out-but-discreet lesbian, I was supposed to infiltrate Ejército de Liberación Nacional. ELN is the National Liberation Army in Colombia, a Marxist guerilla group known for kidnapping foreign businessmen for ransom."

"Really?" Jody looked at her skeptically. "Kidnapping for ransom?"

"I was on the side of the good guys," Tia said in a reassuring tone. "Or I thought I was," she added ruefully.

"What did being a lesbian have to do with the assignment?"

"During the initial surveillance, it was discovered that the wife of the ranking sector lieutenant had a preference for women. I have a deeply rooted Latin heritage. I speak Spanish like a native, and since my sexual orientation is for women, it was decided I was the perfect operative to insinuate myself into her life. And that's what I did. Her name was Maria Maladin, and I may have effortlessly seduced her, but she swept me off my feet."

Jody saw the wistful look in Tia's eyes. "You slept with her?"

"Many, many times."

"Is that expected of all CIA agents on assignment… or just the women?" Jody waited patiently while Tia considered her answer.

"You're expected to do whatever it takes to stay in control of the case. If that involves becoming sexually involved, the unspoken rule is that as long as it doesn't compromise the assignment—"

"How can sex with a suspect not compromise a case?"

"She wasn't a suspect, her husband was, and The Agency can choose to ignore your tactics as long as the results come out in their favor. No one officially ordered me to use sex, but when they picked me for that particular job, it was understood that was what they expected me to do to get into the inner circle."

"So you just followed orders?"

"Not at first. I was pissed that they automatically thought I would sleep with just any woman who was attracted to other women. I told my boss that. I was pissed that they pulled me from a job where I was being really successful and threw me into the middle of another one just because I was gay."

"What changed your mind?"

"Maria." Tia looked contrite. "I got myself invited to a party the Maladins were throwing. I pretended to be a relative of the operative who had been working the case from the start. He knew that Maria collected fine linens, like Victorian lace fans and ribbon cloths, and The Agency made sure he had a varied supply to sell her. That's how he managed to become acquainted with Maria and get onto their estate. Maria was friendly and approachable, to a point, but he wasn't able to do a proper infiltration. Her husband was inaccessible to anyone outside the circle."

Jody tried to suppress the doubts she was having about Tia's narrative. "And that's where you came in?"

"Yes. Maria invited my 'cousin' to a festive event. Some of her relatives were going to be attending, and they wanted to meet the linen peddler." Tia smiled fondly. "He brought me with him. I took one look at that woman, and I thought my body temperature had gone haywire."

"Wow. That beautiful, huh?" Jody sounded jealous.

"It was about more than her being fashion model beautiful. She was... irresistibly exciting. Her intense confidence and power were very sexy in their own right. She was engaging, she was iridescent, she was classy, and oh so deceptively clever. It was rare that Maria didn't get whatever she wanted."

"She wanted you," Jody stated flatly.

"Yes. And I wanted her. It was a week before we were able to be alone and intimate."

"Really. A whole week."

Tia shrugged. "I wasn't exactly playing hard to get. It was a torrid affair. I felt as if the scorching tension between us was probably visible to anyone who happened to be in a room with us. Señor Maladin didn't seem to mind; it kept his wife occupied while he attended to his business."

Jody was incredulous. "You mean he *knew?*"

"I don't see how he couldn't have known. Why does that surprise you? You must know your husband has other women."

Jody sat back in her chair. "Yes. I know about them. But Tony and I aren't in love. I know how possessive men can be, so I'm amazed that this Colombian was okay with it. All male fantasies aside, she was his wife. Did he ever want you to join them in bed?"

"It was never an issue. He had his playmates, and she had hers. Everything fell into place pretty quickly. During pillow talk, Maria told me everything I needed to know."

"Why would she trust you like that?"

"Just like you're asking yourself why should you trust me like that?"

Jody bowed her head, embarrassed. "What am I supposed to say?" She looked up at Tia, her expression soft. "First you tell me that my husband cooked up this scheme to kidnap and kill me for money he doesn't really need, and now you tell me you are ex-CIA.

I want to believe you, Tia. You have to understand how hard it is for me. I don't want to be taken for a fool again."

Tia leaned forward. "I can see this is upsetting you, but as I think you can tell, I really care about you, and I need you to know who I am. I need you to understand what got me to this point in my life. I can't make you believe me. I can only tell you what happened and hope that you do."

The hint of vulnerability in Tia's bearing gave some credence to her sincerity. Jody nodded. "So... Maria... secrets... pillow talk."

Tia studied Jody awhile and then continued. "I became her confidant, her outlet for many things. To others, she referred to me as her personal assistant, and when we weren't burning up the sheets, that's pretty much what I became."

Having experienced Tia's bedroom skills, and visualizing Tia making love to a hot-blooded, gorgeous Latina, Jody was hit with an uncomfortable blend of desire and envy. "Sounds like your assignment really worked out well for you," she said. If Tia noticed her blush, she didn't comment on it.

"At least up to that point. It wasn't only nice, it was flattering to be in bed with someone as seductive as Maria Maladin. She wasn't a novice lover by any means. The more immersed I became in the assignment, the harder I fell for her. My place in her life might have been an act, but the way she made me feel was anything but."

"You were in love with her," Jody said, feeling irrationally covetous.

"Yes."

"I'm guessing it didn't work out the way you hoped it would."

"That was one of the problems. I wasn't sure what I was hoping for. I had broken a cardinal rule by getting personally involved. The only protocol for that was to pull back and get uninvolved."

"So what did you do?"

"I tried to force myself to pull back, and I continued to filter crucial information back to The Agency through the original operative, but other things heated up and it was just too important for me not to stay and see it through."

"What kinds of things?"

"Things with the ELN. Hostilities between them and FARC, the Revolutionary Armed Forces of Colombia, had started to escalate near the Venezuelan border. FARC has been trying to take over ELN's territory there, and the number of kidnappings and massacres was on the rise."

"Massacres?" It was as though Jody suddenly realized the gravity of Tia's former job.

"To show power. To show each other who held the hammer. Maria told me it had gone too far for her liking. Her husband had ordered the kidnapping of some pretty high up U.S. and German oil executives who were scheduled to visit Bogotá for some kind of summit. ELN was already getting money from property taxes and the drug trade, now they were going into extortion. If they could pull it off—and there was no reason to believe they couldn't—it would make them top dogs, as would winning that little territorial civil war along the Orinoco. Maladin had unexpectedly ratcheted everything up to get a jump on the Araucanian sector of FARC and AUC, the Autodefensas Unidas de Colombia." Tia's fervor was clear in her voice as she related the events.

"So what did you do?"

"I continued to play my part and made sure all my intel got passed on. I sat tight and awaited my orders. Then my fellow operative, the guy who sold Maria the collectable linens, blew it. He totally jumped the gun. He screwed up and hung me out to dry. I didn't realize he had been out to get his cachet back ever since they brought me in because of his failure to break into the inner circle."

Jody was riveted. "What happened?"

"Somehow information got into the hands of FARC about what Maladin was planning. Word got around that there was an informant in their midst, someone in or near someone in the inner circle. Maria didn't seem to suspect me, at least not openly, but she and her husband did suspect my co-worker and, since he was allegedly a relative, I was told to call him and ask him to come over, to tell him Maria wanted to place an order. I played dumb, like I had no clue why they really wanted him there. Maria kept me... occupied... the rest of the afternoon so I didn't have a chance to warn him. Meeting time came, and he never showed. All eyes turned to me, and I was escorted to Señor Maladin's study. I'll never forget the look on Maria's face when I left the room."

"Betrayal?"

"Like she had been stabbed in the heart. It was..." Tia looked skyward and then at her fingers that drummed nervously on the table. The words stuck in her throat.

Jody reached over and gently put her hand over Tia's. "What happened?"

"I was burned with my cover blown. I was about to be stuck in Colombia with no way out, so I had nothing to lose. I fought like a tiger and got away from Maladin's men. I had to hide out while I figured out what went wrong and how to get the hell out of South America."

"You mean the CIA just deserted you?" Jody was dubious.

"Yes. HQ was advised I had blown the assignment and that everything that went wrong was my fault, that my arrogance and irresponsibility had compromised the case. The failure of that objective was a huge loss. They had no further use for me. When something like that happens, you no longer exist to The Agency. You're on your own. You're erased."

"But you weren't the one who blew it." Jody sounded indignant enough for both of them.

Tia shrugged in resignation. "My superiors needed a scapegoat. I was the most convenient mark. My supervisor wasn't a fan of mine to begin with, never a supporter of females in The Agency, period, and the operative who blew the case was someone he had mentored. It didn't take a rocket scientist to figure out who was going to be the one deemed culpable."

"Oh God, Tia… that's… that's just not right." She squeezed Tia's hand. "What about Maria? Did you ever see her again?"

"No. It was too dangerous. And, within a week, she was dead."

Jody was stunned. "Dead?"

"She, her husband, and his entourage perished in a suspicious explosion a few days after I left their estate."

"I'm so sorry," Jody said, and clearly meant it. "Do you think it was the CIA?"

"No. I think it was either FARC or United Self-Defense Forces. However, I'll never be convinced that whoever was responsible wasn't tipped off by my co-worker about where the Maladins were going to be that night."

"Seriously? But how did he get away with that?"

"He blamed it on me, and they believed him. And there I was, in Colombia, abandoned by The Agency, and a price on my head from the ELN."

"How did you get out?" Jody's touch was now ice-cold.

"Sheer luck. I had to do some things I'm not exactly proud of to get me across the border, but I'm alive."

"Weren't you afraid?"

"It wasn't the first time I faced my mortality, and I'm positive it won't be the last. You don't go to work for the CIA if you're looking for a stable, secure life."

"Are you afraid now?"

"Only for you," Tia said truthfully.

While Jody sat agape, Tia unraveled the account of Montgomery's entrapment and how she had been blackmailed into the abduction. Jody's sole thought was *Who is this man?* Finally she realized she was staring at Tia, and she closed her mouth and cleared her throat. "Tony murdered a prostitute? With your gun?"

"Yes."

Jody absorbed this with a slight nod and said, "A gun that you kept from when you were a CIA agent."

"Officer," Tia said. "I was a CIA officer. An agent is usually a foreign national. I guess the movies like the sound of 'agent' better than 'officer.'"

"But I still don't understand. How did Tony find you? I mean, how did he know who you were?"

Tia's voice was now raspy, her throat obviously dry. "He told me this Bruce guy who works for him was the one who found me. How Bruce knew who I was, I don't know. He ever mention a Bruce to you?"

Jody searched her memory and shook her head. "Not that I remember. I didn't know he knew anyone named Bruce. But I'm discovering I really didn't know the bastard at all." There was bitterness in her voice.

"Well, whoever this Bruce is, he led your husband to me."

"You can stop referring to him as my husband, because as soon as we figure out what we're going to do, he won't be my husband for long." Jody threaded her fingers through her blonde locks as she slowly processed everything Tia had told her. Finally, she got back to what was most important to her. "Why? Why does Tony want me dead?"

"As to that, I'm not really sure. It seems as if it has something to do with him getting even with your father."

"My father? What could he have possibly done to push Tony to this point?" She abruptly stood. "I really need a drink. Can I get you anything?"

"Oh God, yes."

Chapter 22

Plenty in the purse cannot prevent starvation in the soul.
—Anonymous

Montgomery awoke from a sound night's sleep. His guided tour of the Wainwright yachts had been a success, and everything was going along as smoothly as he could have hoped. Just a day or two more and he would be free and independently rich, without the family ties. He enjoyed toying with one of the wealthiest dynasties in the world, but he was getting bored. It was time to get the ball rolling.

He wondered what was going on at his in-laws' estate, how fervent and frightened John was, and how chafed and indignantly out of her mind Sondra probably was. But before he jumped into that frying pan, he needed to call the killer and then the geek.

Bruce, although obviously very smart, was a moron in Montgomery's book. Bruce bulked up for some woman he didn't even know, got hooked on steroids that made him beholden to punks, and became a victim of his own addictions and low self-esteem. If Montgomery hadn't needed Bruce's computer expertise, he would have eliminated him the second he refused to kidnap and kill Jody.

How fortunate that Bruce had come up with Tia Ramone. The burnt-out alcoholic had been the perfect patsy. He had her between the proverbial rock and hard place where she had to do what he told her. For the once-respected CIA operative, there was no way out. He couldn't afford any witnesses. Both she and Bruce would have to die. Two loners with only enemies. No one would miss them.

Jody had just placed a beer in front of her, and Tia pulled her in for a gentle liplock. Tia's cell phone rang right in the middle of their tender kiss.

"Do you want to listen in on this?" Tia asked.

When Jody hesitated, Tia figured Jody wasn't sure she wanted to hear Tony's voice on the other end of the line. Jody sat down next to Tia. "I'll just sit here." As Tia answered her call, Jody poured champagne into a flute half-filled with orange juice.

"Good morning, Agent Ramone," Montgomery greeted brightly.

"I'm not an agent, you mook. That's FBI. What do you want?"

By Montgomery's sharp intake of breath, Tia could tell he was bristling at the slang insult, but he didn't let his irritation come through in his voice. "First, I'm impressed. It's eight a.m. and you don't sound three sheets to the wind. You actually sound awake and alert."

"Gee, I'm so glad you're pleased." Tia glanced at a tension-filled Jody, winked at her, and smiled. She reached over and curled her fingers around Jody's.

"How's my little scorpion this morning?" His complacent tone was aggravating as hell.

"Your little scorpion?" Tia repeated, puzzled. She saw Jody's eyes close in recognition at the phrase, the term of endearment apparently convincing Jody it was, indeed, her husband on the phone. Tia squeezed Jody's hand in support. If Jody was now convinced her husband was what Tia said he was, she was likely also convinced that Tia was telling the truth about the rest of it.

"I sometimes call her that. Her birth sign is Scorpio."

"Your little scorpion seems fine." She was going to let it go at that, and then she added, "I heard her moaning earlier, she seemed to be in some kind of distress, but I found something to relieve her ache." Tia and Jody exchanged an intimate smile.

"Good, good. Is she sick, or do you think it was just stress?"

"Come on, Montgomery, do you really care?"

"Well, it bothers me to think of her being sick."

"But it doesn't bother you to think of her as being dead?" Tia saw Jody's head bow. Tia tightened her fingers around her lover's in a comforting gesture.

"That's different. You know, you had me going there last night, Ramone. I guess deep down inside, despite my taunting and even knowing your preferences, I really didn't think you'd force my wife to have sex with you. After all, you did have some honor at one time."

Yes, and thanks to your wife, I'm getting it back. "Whatever." She shrugged it off. "What'd you call for? I'd like to get my day started. I have some serious drinking to do."

"I can't imagine what your liver must look like. Okay, on to business. I have another couple sentences and a list of individual words that my wife needs to read to Bruce. Got a pen?"

When Montgomery got to his in-laws that morning, the first thing he heard was that Sondra Wainwright had failed the polygraph the day before. Her results were inconclusive. This news made Montgomery chuckle. He had passed with flying colors, and he was lying through his teeth. His mother-in-law flunked, and the only thing she was guilty of was being a cold bitch.

Montgomery searched out Agent Marciano and put on his best concerned expression. "I just heard my mother-in-law didn't pass her polygraph. What does that mean? She's not involved, is she?"

"I'm sorry, Mr. Montgomery, I can't discuss the results of Mrs. Wainwright's test with you," Marciano said.

"Why? My father-in-law already told me that Sondra—"

"Mr. Montgomery," Marciano said, politely but firmly, "I can't. I'm sorry. What Mr. Wainwright tells you is between the two of you, but I'm not allowed to talk about test results with you."

Montgomery held his hand up in concession. "No, it's okay, I understand. I'm just anxious. It's..." He hesitated for dramatic impact. "Sondra has always hated my wife." He knew Marciano would pick it up from there.

The young FBI agent didn't disappoint; he jumped at the bait. "Mrs. Wainwright hates her own daughter?"

Tia dialed Bruce's number while Jody quietly reread the script her husband had prepared for her.

"I wish there was a way I could let my father know I'm okay." Jody sighed.

"Me, too. Unfortunately—" Bruce answered and Tia spoke into the phone. "Yeah, it's me. She's ready with her dialogue."

"Okay. Put her on."

Tia handed the phone to her new lover and studied the table, considering her options while she listened to Jody recite what was on the paper. When Jody was finished, Tia took the phone back. "Got all that?" she asked.

"Yep."

Tia decided to take the chance. "Bruce... can we talk?"

There was dead silence on the other end of the line and then, "You know my name?"

"It's only fair. You know mine. In fact, you know it so well, you gave it to Montgomery."

"I… uh… look, it was nothing personal, okay? I mean, I don't know you, it's just—"

"Bruce." He sounded apologetic. That was a good sign. "We can talk about that another time. Listen, you know Montgomery is going to kill us both when this is over, if not before, right? He's not going to want any loose ends, and that's exactly what you and I are. We know way too much. And there's nowhere on this planet we could hide where he couldn't find us."

There was a long silence, until finally Bruce said, "What do you want?"

"I want to meet. Can you come here? Without anyone knowing?"

Bruce was still staring at the phone after the call was terminated. That had been unexpected. And a relief. But could he trust Tia Ramone? Probably more than he could trust his boss at this point. Plus, Mrs. Montgomery was right there and heard everything, so clearly she was aware of who was behind her kidnapping and the plan to eliminate her regardless of whether or not the ransom was paid. Why was she still going along with it?

What did Ramone have up her sleeve? What could she possibly suggest that could get them out of this mess? Bruce was desperate enough to find out.

But first, he had a job to do.

"Coffs Harbour, sir," Agent Marciano told Wainwright, in response to the question of where the call was originating.

"Where?" the multibillionaire repeated, his tone a reflection of his hope that this location was more believable than Asia.

"Coffs Harbour. It's in Australia. New South Wales. The coast, sir." Marciano braced himself for the tirade he knew was imminent.

Wainwright took two steps closer to Marciano and put his face right up to the agent's. "Do you believe the kidnappers have taken my daughter to Australia?" He bit off each word.

"Uh, no, sir. It's, um, highly unlikely." Marciano wished he was in Coffs Harbour at the moment, not standing in front of John Wainwright.

"What kind of dog and pony show are you people running around here? I want to know where my daughter is, and I want to know today! Do you understand me, you imbecile?"

"Mr. Wainwright, there's no need for name calling. We're doing our best, sir," Marciano told him as civilly as possible.

"If that's true, then the FBI is in a sorry state. Where is your boss?"

"He had to brief his supervisor in Washington, sir." Marciano checked the time on his watch. "He should be here any minute now."

"Good. When he gets here, maybe he can tell me why his boss in Washington isn't here, directing you inept fools on how to get my daughter back. I want some progress made on this today, or I start handling it myself."

"Sir, as I have advised you—"

"Shut up, Marciano, or I'll have your job."

"Yes, sir." Marciano watched the irate plutocrat stomp away from him. He expelled a deep breath. *You can have my job, and then you'll know what it's like to have to deal with people like you.* He turned back toward the living room and encountered Anthony Montgomery.

"Don't mind him. He's just used to saying 'jump' and having people say 'how high?' I know you guys are doing everything you can. I mean, the whole world's watching, so I know the last thing you want to do is screw up." Montgomery's voice was soothing… in a snake-oil salesman sort of way.

Marciano appreciated that Montgomery was a lot easier to deal with than Wainwright, but that was starting to not sit well with him. Montgomery was almost too easy to deal with. Although he had been nothing but helpful and cooperative, there was something about Montgomery that made the hairs on the back of Marciano's neck stand on end. Maybe he was just overly wary because of the unnecessary dressing down Wainwright had just given him. Montgomery was more solicitous than either Daddy or Mama Wainwright, but then it was his wife who was being held for ransom and having God only knew what being done to her in the interim. That would make any husband crazy.

"How close are we to getting my wife back safely?" Montgomery asked.

That was one of the problems. Montgomery wasn't acting crazy. Marciano studied the man opposite him. He looked too well rested. Marciano made a snap decision. "I don't seem to be giving out the right answers here, and I'm not in charge of the case, so I think from now on, you should probably get your information from Agent Sanborn." With a polite nod, Marciano walked away.

Montgomery cocked his head in curiosity as Marciano moved away from him, and then he shrugged. The agent was probably embarrassed by Wainwright's outburst. Montgomery had tried to reassure Marciano that the old man's hissy fit wasn't personal, but he could understand how a grown man not used to dealing with Wainwright's tantrums would get self-conscious. He'd give Marciano an hour or two and ask again about their progress. He had to plan his next move.

As long as he could make his father-in-law an unwitting participant in the "good cop, bad cop" routine, he was pretty sure Marciano would remain his best bet for inside information. By tomorrow, if the money ball wasn't already rolling, he'd have to raise the stakes. Although it was fun playing the FBI and watching his in-laws squirm, it was getting tedious, and he didn't want the feds to get too close to finding Jody before he eliminated his two accomplices.

Chapter 23

Nothing pleases a little man more than an opportunity to crack a big whip.
　—Anonymous

　　The Quintessence had been easy to find. Bruce had gone to the pier and rented a boat to get out to the yacht for his meeting with the woman hired to abduct and murder Jody Montgomery. Tia Ramone might be setting him up, but he made the trip anyway. If she did plan to kill him, he felt it would be easier to reason with her than with Tony. As he approached the craft, he saw no movement anywhere. He hoped she was just being covert by not showing herself until she was sure of who was approaching the vessel.
　　Bruce tied his small motorboat to the aft deck landing and climbed aboard. He looked around as he reached the top step that led to the bridge. "Hello?" he called out cautiously and walked under the immense radar arch.
　　"Too early for a beer?"
　　The voice behind him was confident and well-modulated. He spun around to see a tall, striking, dark-haired woman. She smirked as she held out a sweating bottle of Corona. "It's never too early for a beer." Bruce focused on the woman who must hate him for what he had gotten her into.
　　Tia removed the cap and handed the bottle to him. "Good. You're my kind of guy. Relatively speaking, of course. Come on." She tilted her head sideways. "Let's go to the salon and meet the Mrs."

　　Bruce felt duly scrutinized as he stood in front of Jody, feeling extremely uncomfortable. The look on her face indicated he wasn't what she had expected. She probably assumed he would be much less husky. Everyone usually did. She also wore an expression that said she had seen him before but couldn't quite place him.

"Where do I know you from, Bruce?"

"I work for your husband, Mrs. Montgomery. I'm his main techie and troubleshooter." Bruce found it just as difficult not to stare at his boss's gorgeous wife as it was the first time he had ever seen her. He guzzled his beer and found interest in the carpet.

"A little thirsty, are you?" Tia asked sarcastically. She took the empty bottle from his hand and replaced it with another cold beer.

"I'm understandably a little nervous." Bruce sat down on the couch.

"I remember where I've seen you," Jody said. "Tony's office, doing something with his hard drive."

Bruce smiled, mildly impressed that she had actually remembered their ten-second encounter. "Yes, that was me."

Tia sat down next to Jody and pinned Bruce with a probing gaze. "How do you know me, Bruce?"

"I don't. Not really." He eyeballed both women and returned his attention to Tia. "How much does Mrs. Montgomery know?"

"I know as much as Tia knows."

Bruce nodded and took a long swig of Corona.

"What I don't know is how I got involved in all this," Tia said. "I'd like to know how that happened, and we would both like to know what your boss has on you that makes you beholden to him. Also, anything you might have on him."

"How would knowing that help anything?" Bruce asked.

"It might not," Tia said. "But the more I know about Montgomery—and I mean every dirty little detail you can tell me—the better chance I have of figuring a way out of this. Because if we can't turn this back on him somehow, we're in deep, deep shit." Tia emptied the contents of her bottle with one long drink. "But whatever else happens, I want to make a pact with you right now that we save Mrs. Montgomery."

Jody placed her hand on Tia's forearm. "I want us all to get out of this alive." She looked deeply into Tia's eyes. "Which is why I didn't run away this morning."

Bruce got the definite impression that Mrs. Montgomery was more than just a hostage to Tia. *Damn. That happened quickly.* Not that Bruce could blame either woman for falling into bed with the other. Tia Ramone was as uniquely extraordinary as Jody Montgomery, and his boss's wife could do a hell of a lot better than what she had. And with Tia trying to save Mrs. Montgomery, and the both of them as well, she obviously wasn't the rogue Montgomery had made her out to be.

"I promise that whatever happens, I'll do what I can to help you save Mrs. Montgomery," Bruce said.

"Please. It's Jody."

Bruce smiled at the captivating heiress and took a deep breath. "Where do I begin…"

Jody sat back in her chair, stunned. Once again she had to ask herself who was this man she had been married to? As Bruce unraveled his tale, she felt a chill unlike any she had ever experienced.

While Bruce spoke, Jody observed Tia. Her captor-turned-lover wore a formidable expression. She was clearly intent on what Bruce had to say.

When he finished, Tia stood. "Why don't you go grab a pair of trunks from the guest closet out on the deck and go for a swim while Jody and I think this through."

Bruce nodded and quickly exited.

Jody rested her head in her hands and sighed. "This just gets worse and worse. Now what?" She glanced up at Tia, who smiled.

"I think we've found our ticket out of this. I'll be right back."

She rose from the table and disappeared into the master stateroom. When she returned, she held the prepaid cell phone Montgomery had purchased for her. Dialing a number from memory, Tia sat down, apparently comfortable and confident enough to wink at Jody. "Special Operations Division," Tia said into the phone. "Yes. Javier Zamora, please. Tell him it's Anna Santiago."

This made Jody sit up and take notice. She mouthed, "Who?"

Tia reached over and patted Jody's hand. "One of my operative aliases, one that my friend will recognize immediately." Suddenly her eyes lit up and she said, "Javier, ¿cómo está?"

"Santa mierda," Zamora said, taking her lead and communicating with her entirely in Spanish. "Do you know how many people are looking for you? What the fuck did you get yourself into? Offing a streeter with Agency heat?"

"Are you on a secure line?"

"Secure as it can get in this place. Where are you?"

"Let's talk business first. I'm calling in that debt."

There was dead silence on the other end of the line. "You can't do this to me, T... Anna. I cannot get caught up in your little problem. I know what I promised you, I haven't forgotten, but you're persona non grata around here. I know I owe you, but let's be realistic. It ain't gonna be happening now." Naturally, his instinct was for self-preservation, first and foremost. "You would have to have a pretty powerful reason for me to stick my neck out for you right now."

"I do. *My* neck is on the line. If you don't help me, I'm dead. Not only can you save my life here, I have a career maker for you, compadre. You know the top story on the news right now?"

"Yeah, the heiress thing. You got something on that?"

"You could say that. Actually, I have possession of a certain package."

It took Zamora a moment to respond. "You—you what?" His tone was one of disbelief. "You mean you actually have *the package?*"

"Yes. But, Javi, I have something to barter to get myself out of this jam—"

"Jam? Jam? You call what you're in a jam?" He laughed. "You always were one for minimizing things. Jesus Christ, Anna. I can't believe you're involved in any of this. What were you thinking! Let me ask, is the package damaged in any way?"

Tia grinned and switched to English. "No. The package is perfect. In fact, I'm admiring its beauty right now." Jody blushed and looked away. Tia returned to speaking Spanish. "She is alive and well, and pissed off, but not at me. Would you like to speak to her?"

He hesitated, apparently confused. "No. So you're not... uh... holding onto the package, awaiting payment?"

"No. I'm keeping the package safe."

There was another contemplative pause. "What about the prostitute in the car?"

"Unfortunate, but I didn't kill her, and I can tie that incident to this one."

"I knew you'd hit rock bottom, but I didn't think you'd resort to killing someone who didn't try to kill you first. Not your style. So, you've really got something for me?"

"Something big, my friend."

"Give me ten minutes, and then I want you to call me at this number." He gave her the number of his personal cell phone.

Tia snapped the phone shut triumphantly. "We're in." She had no doubt Javier would come through for her. He was DEA, and he and Tia had become close while working on a project together. She had saved his life. They were leaving their debriefing in Ciudad Juárez when Tia spotted the laser dot targeting Javier's head. She tackled him and slammed him to the ground a millisecond before a rapidly fired succession of bullets pierced the building sign behind them. Tia had always believed that she was also scoped that day, and had she not noticed the intense red spot that marked Javier for death, neither of them would have made it to their vehicles alive.

Zamora swore he owed her and would never refuse any request, regardless of how she needed to cash in on his promise. Tia hadn't intended to ever collect on the debt, but she never anticipated a circumstance like the one she was now in. Had Bruce not opened up about the drug aspect, Tia would have still been trying to come up with a way to save them all without asking for Javier's help.

"You want to clue me in here, Anna?" Jody reached into the refrigerator and pulled out another beer for Tia and a champagne split for herself.

"Sure. In 2005, I was in Central America, just before my last assignment in Colombia, by coincidence. I fell into a situation that allowed me to assist the DEA on a project called Operation Flexión. It was a twenty-one-month investigation, and I only came in on the tail end."

She popped the tab on the can and took a refreshing swig. "Operation Flexión was a task force that targeted major steroid manufacturing companies, their owners, and their trafficking associates. Over eighty percent of the steroids seized were from Colombia. Although these companies conducted their business over the Internet, they also supplied numerous pharmacies along the Mexican border towns, where U.S. customers could buy steroids and smuggle them back across the border into the United States." Tia took a swig, then drew the cold can across her heated forehead and touched it to the back of her neck. "That's where I met Javier. He and I were selected from our respective agencies to assist the South American Federal Agency of Investigation."

Jody popped the cork off the bottle and poured it into a glass with some remaining mimosa. "I didn't realize the steroid trade was such a problem."

"Just those nine companies had average combined sales totaling seventy-five-million dollars a year. That may be a drop in the bucket to your family, but that's pretty big business in the illicit anabolic steroid world. And that was just online."

"Seventy-five-million dollars isn't a drop in anyone's bucket. How did they think they were going to get away with it?"

"The manufacturers we investigated tried to disguise the marketing of their product by saying it was being developed for use in animals, but the *laboratorios* knew their real customers were anybody from street level dealers to high-end businessmen, like your husband. And they didn't fool the DEA, either. It would be my guess that most of Tony's transactions have been through the Internet. If that's true, the evidence will still be on his hard drive. With Bruce's help, we're going to bring Tony down."

"If Tony had anything illegal on his computer, he's too smart to have left it there. Of that much, I'm sure," Jody said.

"Actually, that's not true." Bruce was walking up the steps, toweling himself off. His sculpted muscles and well-defined abs were quite impressive. Even Tia gave his body a second look. "I just cleaned up his hard drive the other day. He was afraid the FBI was going to seize his computer to see whether there was anything that related to your kidnapping. He ordered me to make everything disappear."

"I didn't think you could do that... erase the hard drive," Jody said.

"You can and you can't. You can't really remove data, but you can make it extremely difficult for anyone to find what they're looking for, even if they're highly skilled. And that's what I did. I wiped his drive and did a multiple encryption. If they do seize his computer, all they'll initially find is legitimate, work-related data."

Tia sat erect, intensity crackling from her every pore. "Bruce, what did you do with all that information you removed? Tell me you saved everything, that you didn't destroy any of it." Tia held her breath. She might be able to tie Tony into the murder of Roxi, might be able to nail him for being the mastermind behind his wife's abduction, but without the evidence on his computer, Javier would have nothing to prove Tony's importation and distribution of illegal steroids. Corroboration of drug sales would be the nail in Montgomery's coffin; without it, the nail would be in hers.

The look in Tia's eyes was suddenly deadly and its import was clear. Bruce swallowed convulsively. "I have to tell you, you're expecting a lot. I mean, come on, if Tony ever finds out I didn't destroy all of that incriminating information, I'll be a walking corpse."

Tia's fists clenched and she rose out of her chair, which prompted him to clarify. "But I saved it all. I have it in a fireproof safe under some floorboards in my apartment." He waved a hand. "I figured if I abruptly disappeared or was found dead during or after this little deal, he wouldn't get away with it. I have a timed message on my pc that will automatically send to the local FBI office if my computer isn't touched over a three-day period."

Tia sat down with a relieved thump. She tilted her head back and ran both hands through her hair. She sighed audibly. "What did your email say?"

"That Tony was behind the kidnapping, that he set us both up and how he did it, and where to find the evidence regarding his illegal drug business."

"So, you were also pretty sure he was going to kill us," Tia said.

Bruce rolled the towel and slung it over his shoulders. "It's always been in the back of my mind, but it never really surfaced as a reality until you said it. I mean, I took the precaution, but it was honestly just that. The practical me figured it was a probability, and the theoretical me kept saying, 'But I'm doing him a favor, I'm working with him on this, he'll leave me alone.' The lure of the money was a big deal for me, and that's all I was focused on because Tony made it as impossible for me to refuse, as he did for you." He looked at Jody. "I'm so very sorry. It wasn't personal."

Tia nodded. "It wasn't personal for Montgomery, either. That's what makes it so wrong, on every level."

Jody shook her head. "I can't believe I've been married to such a monster."

"Neither can I." Tia was sincerely grateful she had been the one chosen to be Jody's executioner, and that she'd had the presence of mind to realize what an absolute prize this woman was. Tony was an idiot. It would give Tia great pleasure to be instrumental in destroying his life, thereby saving hers and Jody's.

Montgomery wondered whether his charm was just the slightest bit off. Agent Marciano was obviously avoiding him, although he assumed that was the result of Marciano's not-so-private dressing down and the agent's resultant discomfort. John didn't seem to appreciate his company today, either, and Sondra never appreciated it, so that was nothing new. She was as disdainful as ever.

The staff was jumpy and, most of all, melancholy. Jody was always a welcome breath of fresh air in her parents' home; the Wainwright employees loved her. Even they weren't responding to Tony's usual appeal. If things didn't improve, he would wind up in a bad mood. Tony hated bad moods. And if he slipped into his dark side, somebody would suffer.

The news networks were set up and fine-tuned for the morning press conference where Walt Sanborn would update the media with only the information the participating law enforcement agencies wanted released to the public. By the end of the day, the response, "We are not at liberty to discuss that at this time," would not satisfy the voracious curiosity of the news hounds. When investigative reporters started to poke around where their noses didn't belong, Tony knew things could get complicated for him.

Just before the daily media feeding frenzy began, the family gathered stoically behind the assortment of public information officers who would take turns speaking and answering questions. Danny Marciano quietly approached Montgomery.

"We're going to have to confiscate your office computer and your secretary's computer."

Had they suddenly found something, or did they think they had? Montgomery choked down his concern and nodded amiably. "No problem." If they were just following procedure, they should have impounded his computer when they seized Jody's. Marciano had advised him they might take possession of his computer; that was the reason Bruce had erased his hard drive. It was the look in Marciano's eyes that made Montgomery uneasy. He tried to appear nonchalant, but he calculated the minutes until the press conference would be over so he could contact Bruce, just to be assured the authorities would find nothing incriminating. He took a couple of deep breaths, swallowed his paranoia, and put on his best game face for the cameras.

Marciano was sure they would find nothing of interest on the computer, otherwise Montgomery wouldn't have been so accommodating, but something about Montgomery tugged at him. Or maybe Marciano was just peeved because he and his co-workers were doing the best they could to bring the situation to a satisfactory conclusion, and still he got his ass chewed. He wasn't even in charge of anything, and he was taking the heat. He knew that was only because he had been convenient, a body at whom Wainwright could vent. The man wanted his daughter back, and Marciano was positive Wainwright had no qualms about paying the money that would bring her back safely.

Mrs. Wainwright, on the other hand, was a contemptible piece of work. Even though the result of her polygraph was inconclusive, instinct told him she had nothing to do with her daughter's abduction, despite Montgomery's effort to direct suspicion her way. The woman just embodied the word Bitch. Marciano had no doubt that this woman had no love for anything except her husband's bank account. Her behavior and attitude were clearly reprehensible, but that aside, the agent didn't think Mrs. Wainwright was smart enough to pull off a kidnapping and not get caught. Plus, it would have required way too much effort on her part.

The first rule of procedure was to look at the spouse, and Marciano hoped that's what his superiors were doing. Neither Montgomery nor his secretary had been near their office computers since the FBI became involved in his wife's abduction. Although either one or both could have added or deleted information from remote locations, FBI technicians could almost certainly recover anything that had been changed. Commandeering the equipment at this particular time was mostly for effect, and Marciano especially wanted to monitor Montgomery's response. He couldn't put his finger on what it was he was looking for, nor did he have anything solid to go on, but the feeling in his bones about Anthony Montgomery was suddenly not a good one.

Chapter 24

The heaviest thing a person can carry is a grudge.

—Anonymous

At first dubious, Javier Zamora listened patiently as Tia untangled her recent saga for him. If he hadn't known Tia so well, he would have accused her of being overly dramatic, but what she told him was too outrageous not to be true. His enthusiasm grew with each word, and his imagination reveled in the glory and recognition this could bring him. When she was done and he had written everything down, Zamora asked, "What do you want out of this, other than the obvious?"

"What's the obvious? To get my reputation back? My job back? It's too late for my reputation. Whatever they didn't fuck up, I did, and I don't want to go back and work for The Agency. But I do want to be exonerated. An apology would be nice, but I'm not going to hold my hand over my ass waiting for that. Unfreezing my accounts would be appreciated... and I want immunity for Bruce. Anything else, I'll have to think about."

"I'll look into the immunity thing, but—"

"Don't 'but' me, Javi. This guy is handing you Montgomery's head on a platter. It's the least you can do for him, besides putting him in witness protection when this is done." She winked at Bruce, who looked astonished and relieved. "You'll probably get a promotion and a big, fat raise out of it."

"God, I'm hoping. I'm going to contact FININT, too," Zamora said, referring to Financial Intelligence. "Any idea how he planned on moving the ransom money?"

"According to Bruce, Montgomery's been putting all the money from his side business into offshore accounts. He was going to work the ransom money through those same channels—make anonymous deposits in Antilles, have it transferred to the Cayman

Islands, and then transfer it to Singapore. The banks in Singapore have the easiest deposit and withdrawal procedures and are protected by bank secrecy laws."

"Ah. Their trust-based system leaves no paper trail."

"Exactly."

"And people say crime doesn't pay." Zamora snorted. "He could spend all of it and no one would be the wiser. No repercussions."

"Yes. Honestly, Javi, I don't think this is really about the money. Maybe the drugs are, but not the abduction. He's disgruntled. He's got a grievance against his father-in-law, and this is his way of really hurting the old man."

"At the expense of his wife's life? Cold bastard."

"He really is."

"Tia, we really need something to put Montgomery in that vehicle to connect him to the prostitute's murder. Otherwise it's your word against his."

"And Bruce's."

"Bruce wasn't there, so his word on that is hearsay. I read the report. They found no identifiable fingerprints in the car other than those of the owner who reported it stolen, yours, and the victim's. Lots of smears. And very little blood."

She bolted upright. "That's it! Javier, have them check the blood found in the car. Montgomery cut his chin on the gun sight when we struggled as he got into the car. Roxi's blood was there, of course, so maybe forensics missed it. Montgomery's face bled quite a bit. See if any of it got anywhere other than on himself."

"I believe they found a spot or two of dried blood on the back of the driver's headrest that hasn't been identified. I'll see if the FBI has taken Montgomery's DNA. If they haven't, they'll get it."

"Could you make sure they do that without tipping him off as to why they want it? We don't need him to suddenly disappear so that we're all looking over our shoulders for the rest of our lives. We don't know who he may have on his payroll."

"Don't worry. Just leave it to me."

"If anyone else said that to me, believe me, I'd be worrying. I'm trusting you to bring us all home on this, Javi."

"You know I will."

"Call me at this number when you have something," Tia said.

"Isn't Montgomery tracking your minutes? Won't he want to know if you've used time that wasn't spent talking to him?"

"He might be, but my guess would be that he'll think I've been talking to Bruce. If he asks, I'll just tell him it took us a few tries to get Jody to say her lines the way he wanted."

"For your sake, I hope he buys it."

"I don't think it will be an issue."

"Okay," Zamora said, "let me get started on this. I'll keep you posted. Thank you very much, Tia. You've made my day. Hell, fuck that. I think you just made my career."

"Don't get cocky on me, Javi. Just nail the prick, and let's all get on with our lives."

Zamora laughed. "I see you still minimize things."

Tia snapped the phone shut and placed it on the table. She smiled confidently as she looked at Jody. "Tell me, does Tony have fire insurance? Because he'll need it where he's going when he dies."

In spite of the gravity of the situation, Jody smirked. "Knowing him, he probably sold a policy to Satan." She shook her head. "Just listening to you makes my head spin. All that shifting of money. It's so complicated."

"That's the idea. It's not supposed to be easy to trace back to its origin."

Bruce rubbed his eyes and looked at Tia. "Do you think your friend can really get me out of this?"

"With everything I just gave him, if he can't, no one can."

"Tia, I'm so sorry I involved you in this. I can't believe you don't want to hang me out to dry," Bruce said.

"Well, Bruce, I look at it this way. This was a wake-up call if ever I needed one. And besides, if I hang you out to dry, I tighten my own noose as well."

"Will I owe you now?"

"If we all get out of this alive and things work out the way I think they will, I'd say we can call it even."

Bruce's phone rang, and he glanced at the Caller ID. "Shit. It's Tony. He shouldn't be calling me. I wonder what's happened." Bruce stood up and walked away from the women to take the call.

Both women studied his body language. Jody kept her voice quiet. "If your standing with The Agency was still valid, could you personally arrest Tony?"

"No," Tia said.

"Why not?"

"Because the CIA is a foreign intelligence agency, not a law enforcement agency. Making arrests or conducting investigations of domestic subjects on domestic soil is the FBI's job." Reading the worry in Jody's expressive blue eyes, Tia slid her hand over and laced her fingers with Jody's. "We'll get him, and this will all be over."

Jody looked down at their joined hands. "All of it?"

Tia reached over to lift Jody's chin with her free hand. When she had totally engaged Jody's eyes with her own, she said, "I think there's at least one thing that merits further investigation."

A smile lit Jody's face. "I'd really like that."

Bruce felt some satisfaction at the worry in Montgomery's voice as he repeated, "You're sure they won't see anything suspicious on my computer?"

"They might be able to tell it has been recently wiped down. Just say you had an intrusion scare with a hacker. Working in the field you do, you store information on your hard drive that's very sensitive, and it should make sense to them that you would have to do that. If they need to know more, point them in my direction and I'll confirm your story."

"I don't want them anywhere around you, Bruce. I don't want you connected to this at all unless it's absolutely necessary. Those boys start sniffing around you, and everything might unravel. I can't take that chance."

Bruce was almost hurt by Montgomery's lack of faith in him. "You might not have a choice."

"Where are you? Sounds like seagulls in the background."

Bruce thought quickly. "I'm at the pier. I thought I'd come down to the beach and have a quick swim and then pick up some fish for dinner. Davy Jones' Locker has the best fresh catches in town."

"You're buying your fish at Davy Jones' Locker? I'm paying you too much."

Bruce could hear the smile in Tony's voice. "Probably." Bruce was relieved that Tony believed him. His fears were also eased by the fact that his boss wasn't computer savvy. He could tell Montgomery anything he wanted to regarding the technology, and Montgomery would question him only minimally. As of that morning, he was no longer intimidated by Anthony Montgomery. He realized he now held the hammer that could smash his boss's head. He wished he didn't have to leave the yacht until Montgomery had been caught.

"So, tell me, how does my wife sound? Scared?"

Bruce improvised. "Of course she sounds scared. She has no idea what's going on, and she has a psycho watching over her. It took her a few tries to get her script to sound right."

"You know, since she's going to die anyway, maybe I should visit her one last time. It won't matter whether or not she knows everything just before she dies."

"Your wife is beautiful, Tony. I don't understand why you need to kill her. It's such a waste."

"It's about power, Bruce. It's about who has the most influence and authority. Greatness isn't about being strong, Bruce, it's about how you use your strength."

"I guess that makes sense." Now that he had gotten to know Jody a little better, Bruce hated Montgomery even more.

"Of course it does. Pay attention to me, Bruce. You'll learn a lot."

"I've learned a lot already."

"I need to get back to the main house, see what's happening. I'll be calling you tonight or tomorrow."

"When are we going to wrap this up?"

"Now you sound like Ramone. Soon. This will be over soon."

The finality in the voice made Bruce shiver. He knew exactly what his boss meant.

Bruce walked back to the two women. "They seized his office computer, and he freaked out a little."

"I'm surprised they didn't do that the first day," Tia said. "What will they find on it?"

"Nothing but MediMont business. But they'll be able to see it's been messed with recently, which will raise a big red flag."

"Does he know that?" Jody asked.

"Yes. I told him to tell them he had a hacker intrusion and he had to protect the privacy of his clientele."

"You know they won't buy that," Tia said.

"Yeah, but he did, and right now that's all that matters."

Several hours after he arrived at the Wainwright estate, Agent Walter Sanborn received an urgent message to return to his main office. He couldn't have been more grateful. It had been an uncomfortable day. John Wainwright had chewed him out in front of his subordinates, and Sanborn was still silently fuming. Agent

Danny Marciano, a sharp kid who hadn't been with the Bureau long, tried to give him a head's up but he had blown him off. After he found out that Marciano had also been humiliated in front of anyone within earshot, he decided to give the young agent a break. He requested that Marciano accompany him back to headquarters.

"Sir, may I speak frankly?" Marciano asked, once they had left the estate.

"Please."

"I have a bad feeling about Montgomery."

Sanborn pursed his lips. He also had a bad feeling about the husband, but he couldn't put his finger on any reason why, especially since Montgomery kept coming up clean. However, he knew that gut instinct was an insight to be nurtured in his profession. Too many people went by the book, and too few trusted their intuition. Maybe Marciano could give him some perspective. "Talk to me, Danny."

"I don't have anything concrete, sir. There's just something about him that makes my skin crawl. He's too calm, too smooth. His reactions feel practiced. And today, after the press conference, after I told him we were confiscating his office computer, he took a long walk on the grounds and spoke on his cell phone."

"Pull his cell records."

"We did. There were no pings from his personal cell phone. I can only assume he was speaking on a prepaid wireless, sir."

"Well now, that's interesting. I wonder why he did that."

"Exactly my thoughts, sir."

"Let's see what the regional office has to say."

Javier Zamora had not been looking forward to the meeting with his supervisor. He didn't yet have any conclusive, concrete evidence against Montgomery, though he had set some avenues of investigation in motion. With a sigh, he launched into his report.

"I processed all of the paperwork and pulled all of Montgomery's files, including the records of his last medical check-up. There was no DNA. Also, Montgomery's DNA is not on record with the government or anywhere else we could think of to check. It's going to be complicated to try and match the two spots of blood discovered in the backseat. If we arrest Montgomery now, his lawyer will have him out on bail before we can finish analyzing the computer data I received this afternoon." He hitched his chair closer to the desk.

"The good news is we have probable cause for a warrant. A new confidential informant puts Montgomery at the scene of the prostitute's murder, and that may well tie into the kidnapping of Jody Montgomery."

"Why haven't you turned this information over to the FBI and let them deal with it?"

"It might be connected to something bigger, something that's more in the jurisdiction of the DEA. I would appreciate the latitude to explore the possibility."

"I don't know that I need the headache of possible interagency squabbling over whose case this should be." Zamora waited nervously as his supervisor considered and at last capitulated. "I'll give you twenty-four hours, but you need to bring the FBI up to speed and keep them in the loop."

Elated, Zamora went back to his office and called an associate who gave him the name of a trustworthy higher-up in the Bureau. Zamora contacted him, gave him enough information to get the FBI agent salivating, and asked for some good people who wouldn't tip their hand.

After Bruce left *The Quintessence*, he went to his apartment. He opened his safe, took one set of the discs that held the evidence against his boss to keep for himself, and got the remaining copies ready to hand over to the DEA. He called Javier Zamora to confirm that he had assembled the proof they needed to nail Montgomery, and he arranged a meeting to deliver the incriminating CDs.

"And this is all of it?" Zamora asked as he accepted the large manila envelope from Bruce. He opened the envelope and touched each disc as he counted them.

"Yes." Bruce didn't think twice about lying. Agent Zamora might be on his side, but that didn't mean Zamora's boss or colleagues were. Important evidence could get "lost," depending on who kissed whose ass in that town. Bruce wanted to make sure all the evidence was available to him for his own protection, should Montgomery somehow slither his way out of the impending charges. "So, what happens now?"

"I'll have our tech team review the information on these discs so we can sort out the appropriate charges. If, for some reason, we can't connect Montgomery to the kidnapping, we'll at least have him on the drug counts."

"You will get him, though, right? Because otherwise his attorney will have him out in minutes, and he'll make it his mission to hunt me down and kill me."

Zamora resealed the manila envelope and focused on Bruce. "We'll get him."

"Because he could order me killed, too. It wouldn't give him the same satisfaction, but, you know, dead is still dead." Bruce wiped his sweaty palms on his jeans.

"Relax. The paperwork is already being prepared. We just need to verify this data and log it into evidence."

"What about the kidnapping?"

"We're working on that. With this," Zamora said and held up the envelope for emphasis, "we'll have enough to arrest him and hang onto him until we can file the additional charges."

"And then I can fade into obscurity?"

"You'll be given a new identity and a new town to live in. Whether or not you successfully fade into obscurity will be up to you. You'll have federal protection until the trial."

"What about afterwards?"

"Once Montgomery has been prosecuted and is permanently behind bars, you shouldn't need protection."

"Tony's got a memory like a fucking elephant, and he's a vengeful guy. I don't think he'll stop just because he's incarcerated. I don't think you have any idea the magnitude of the tsunami this will cause."

Zamora smiled. "Montgomery isn't as big as he thinks he is. Believe me, he'll have enough to contend with once he gets to the penitentiary. By the time he makes enough friends to even think about arranging any retaliation, he won't have any idea where to begin looking for you. If he thinks his current clientele will be loyal enough to track you down for him, he'll be unpleasantly surprised."

"Why?"

"Because there'll still be a demand for the drugs, but no supply. They won't care why it's not there anymore, just that it isn't, and they'll be off to find another supplier as soon as possible. Montgomery's regional reign will be over. He'll be replaced. And all his assets will be completely frozen, so if he can't pay to have you found, he won't be able to go after you."

"I don't know." Bruce shook his head. "He can be a pretty charming guy when he wants something."

"Mr. Wechsler, you've been to jail. I realize you didn't experience the caliber of inmates you find at a federal level, but you've had a taste of how the system works. Montgomery's not used to being low man on the totem pole. His charm and good looks could work more against him than for him... at least until he earns his way up that nasty little ladder to the top. By then, I think he'll have more to contend with than you." Zamora placed the envelope in his shoulder briefcase. "Too bad you can't get the millions your boss promised you, huh?"

"Are you kidding? I just want to walk away alive, with a good chance of staying that way, and hopefully, I won't screw up again. I'm getting a second chance. How many people in the depths of hell can say that?" Bruce's "new life" would mean he would have to get off the steroids and return to being the skinny, unpopular geek he once was. Too bad Mrs. Montgomery wasn't going to need a computer nerd at her beck and call. It didn't matter that she wouldn't look at him twice that way. He suddenly felt that she and Tia Ramone would be the only two people who would ever understand and appreciate him.

"You can thank Tia Ramone for that," Zamora said with a wry smile.

"I already did." Bruce actually sounded grateful. Tia Ramone. Boy, what a thunderbolt she turned out to be. He had accessed a majority of Tia's history and knew her capabilities, knew that regardless of his physical strength, she could turn him into cat food with little effort. She should have been furious with him, and yet she was ready to wipe the slate clean in exchange for his help. Instead of detonating, she had been the calm force that said, "Together we can save all our asses."

She would probably never realize what an inspiration she had been to him in just the short time they had interacted. Maybe someday he would have the chance to tell her.

Bruce glanced at the two U.S. Marshals who would be guarding him until the trial, thankful that he was in Tia Ramone's good graces. The marshals might be able to protect him from Montgomery and his associates, but he had no doubt they would have been insufficient to deflect an attack by Tia Ramone.

At the weather-beaten, eleven-story city building that housed the regional FBI offices, Sanborn and Marciano walked quickly to their field manager's office. They closed the door behind them and faced three men: their boss, their boss's boss, and an unfamiliar third person.

"This is Javier Zamora," Russ Morven, the field manager, said. "He's DEA. He needs our help with an assignment. He also has some intel on the Montgomery kidnapping."

"Mrs. Montgomery is safe," Zamora said. "She's under the protection of a colleague of mine." He glared at Sanborn and Marciano. "That information doesn't leave this office." He watched the two men intently; their reaction to that restriction was vital. They looked sincerely relieved, which assuaged any reservations he'd had about sharing additional information.

Marciano jumped into the silence. "Where is she?"

"Not important at this time. Just know that she is alive and well and will cooperate with us completely." Zamora thought that the last thing this kid would want to hear was that she was on a boat he had personally checked.

"When was she rescued, sir?" Sanborn asked Morven.

"She has actually been in the safety of my colleague since the day of her abduction," Zamora answered before Morven could speak.

"What?" Sanborn and Marciano said in unison.

"Why weren't we told?" The frustration was clear in Sanborn's tone. He looked at his boss, who nodded toward Zamora, deferring to the DEA agent.

"We couldn't compromise her welfare by tipping off the person responsible," Zamora said. "Mrs. Montgomery has been going along with everything until we have enough evidence to bring her home safely."

"Can I ask why the DEA is suddenly involved in this?" Sanborn asked. "Last I heard, they didn't get involved in abductions unless they were somehow drug-related."

"That's right."

The set of Zamora's jaw made it clear there would be no further information forthcoming. There was an awkward silence until Marciano said, "Please, please tell me you suspect her husband is involved."

Zamora looked at him sharply." Why do you say that?"

Marciano glanced around the room. The eyes he saw were inquisitive, not angry. He shrugged. "I just don't like the guy. I mean, he's cooperative, and personable enough, but… I don't know. Something just doesn't set right with me."

"As well it shouldn't," Zamora said.

Chapter 25

If you can't be content with what you have received, be thankful for what you have escaped.
—Izaak Walton

The sun settled on the horizon as Jody and Tia silently watched from the foredeck. Jody sat on the padded bench seat between Tia's legs, her feet propped up while she leaned back against the solid body. Tia's arms fastened around Jody's waist, lips occasionally grazing her neck and hair as dark gold, russet, scarlet, and violet painted the sunset.

When darkness covered them, Tia sparked Jody's libido to full flame. Jody was still amazed that someone, anyone, could arouse such a strong reaction from her. As sexually vulnerable as she was feeling, she had also never felt as safe and secure as she did when she was in Tia's embrace. She found that disconcerting and reassuring at the same time.

Everything was happening quickly, but that didn't make it feel any less right. She felt as though she was meant to be in the arms of Tia Ramone. Jody indulged in the pleasure of Tia's hands and lips freely exploring wherever they could reach, and the two women remained in that position until the full moon and the constellations were the only illumination in the cloudless sky.

"Jody?" Tia whispered in Jody's ear after gently nibbling on her lobe.

"Yes?" Jody responded breathlessly.

"Let's go downstairs to the master stateroom. I'm aching to make love to you."

"I don't want to go anywhere. Make love to me here, under the stars." Jody's eyes were dark with need and desire.

"Yessss." Tia turned Jody in her arms and pulled Jody on top of her. Their eager lips met in a deep, passionate kiss. The touch of

Tia's lips to hers sent a jolt directly to Jody's center and started a tingling deep in her belly, almost frightening in its intensity. Jody quivered. She had read about lovers experiencing this type of reaction together, but she'd thought it was just a fantasy created by an author. Until now.

As Jody's tongue lovingly sparred with Tia's, she briefly speculated about what, other than the phenomenal sex, drew her to this woman. They really had nothing in common. Their cultural backgrounds were miles apart, Tia was of an entirely different mindset and financial class, and... *Ohhh, God, when the hell did Tia slide her fingers there?* Jody broke the kiss and gasped for breath as Tia expertly worked her fingers over Jody's sensitive center. The position was awkward for Tia, but she manipulated her fingers knowledgeably. "Jesus, Tia," Jody said, panting as the electricity radiated through her nether regions. She could feel her wetness soaking them both.

"All that moisture for little ol' me?" Tia said playfully, her voice husky.

Jody buried her face into Tia's shoulder and concentrated on the sensations building within her. But just when Jody thought Tia should be circling faster, her lover slowed her pace. "Wh... why are you stopping?" Jody asked in short puffs of breath. "I'm so close... so close..." She rocked against Tia's fingers, trying to regain the rhythm.

"I'm not stopping," Tia murmured.

Jody was thankful she was wearing just a bathrobe she had donned after a quick shower earlier. Tia pushed the open robe off Jody's shoulders with her unoccupied hand, and Jody shed the rest of the terrycloth garment, leaving herself completely naked. When Jody began to sit up, Tia stopped her without altering her cadence.

"Don't. I want you close to me when you come. I want to see your face, your expression." She pulled Jody to her and their gazes locked, neither taking her eyes off the other.

"Please. Faster."

"No," Tia said. "I want you slow and steady. I don't just want to get you off, I want it to build within you. And I want to watch that happen in your eyes."

Jody's breath caught at the impossibly sexy growl in Tia's voice. Tia's index and middle fingers methodically stroked with just enough pressure to incite her clit. Jody's heartbeat accelerated, and she was about to climax, when Tia again reduced her speed. "Oh, fuck, what are you doing?" Jody asked, simultaneously loving and hating Tia's ministrations.

"You'll see." Tia cupped Jody's butt with her other hand and forced Jody's lower body tightly to her own, trapping her talented hand between them. She used the pads of two fingers with decreased pressure, making only the minutest of movements. "Right there?"

"A little to the... Oh God, yes! *Right there.*" It was as though Tia had pressed a magic button. The angle and the leverage of her fingers, along with the suddenly increased pace, made Jody erupt. She almost closed her eyes to ride out her orgasm, but Tia lightly nipped Jody's chin to get her attention. Jody watched Tia's expression through every nuance of the climax. It made Jody come harder and longer than she ever had before.

Bruce was escorted back to his apartment, where he grabbed one of his laptop computers and a couple of changes of clothes and accompanied the assigned U.S. Marshals to a motel room for the night. He wasn't sure what was going to go down, but he was glad he didn't have to be anywhere on Montgomery's radar when the shit hit the fan.

The marshals took up posts outside of the room, while Bruce stretched out on his hard hotel bed and clicked the remote until he found a news station. The same kidnapping-related film loop of Montgomery's studiously grim face on CNN's Headline News every fifteen minutes gave him an upset stomach. He surfed the channels and settled on reruns of *Frasier*. It was the Valentine's Day episode, and Bruce laughed hysterically at the beginning, thinking it was the funniest five minutes on television, ever. Niles was just hilarious. Watching *Frasier* was much better than watching the news.

"Ooooooooh." Jody inhaled as one skilled finger entered her, then another. "Ohhhhhhhhh, God, Tia... faster... harder..." She couldn't take much more of the sweet, exquisite torture. Her body screamed for respite. She had climaxed repeatedly, to the point where she had almost passed out once. Jody had to give back at some stage, but the thought of Tia bucking and writhing underneath her brought Jody to the brink again. Stretched, well lubricated with her own juices, aching and ready, Jody asked for a third finger. Then a fourth. Jody rode Tia's hand only briefly before she cried out her release. She breathlessly collapsed into strong, warm arms that enveloped her protectively.

"Madre de Dios, estas muy seductora," Tia said throatily, holding Jody to her, kissing exposed flesh. "Tienes un cuerpra tan seductora y un alma muy hermosa. Si pudeira venir a casa cada noche , te juro que no estaria donde estoy. Creo que podria amar te, mi magnifica."

"God, it is so sexy when you whisper Spanish in my ear. What are you saying?" When Tia was silent, Jody lifted her head to look into her eyes. "Tell me. Please?"

Tia repeated it in English. "Mother of God, you are so seductive. You have such a seductive body and such a beautiful soul. If I could come home to you every night, I swear I wouldn't be where I am. I believe I could love you, my magnificent one."

Jody played with a strand of Tia's silky, long black hair. "Thank you. So... um... you would really want to come home to me every night?"

The question was asked with such a sense of modesty and humility, Tia's heart began to pound. Jody's absence of vanity and self-importance was one of the reasons Tia responded to her so fervently. "Jesus, Jody, are you kidding? Who in their right mind wouldn't want to be with you?"

"Other than my own husband?"

"I said 'in their right mind.' He's a fucking idiot. And, come on, you never really loved him anyway. You were accommodating your parents. Now it's time for you. Just because he had his own agenda is no reason for you not to fully explore what you've discovered and acknowledged about yourself."

"What about you?"

"Me? Right now I think I'm suffering a severe case of inflammation of the wishbone."

"While I think I want my life to include you in it. In fact"— Jody gave Tia a heated kiss—"I know I do."

"We'll talk about that, okay? I have a lot to come to terms with, a lot to figure out. I don't know how I could possibly be good for you."

"Can I be the judge of that?"

Tia adjusted her position over Jody. "Can we discuss this later? Right now, I kind of have this crisis that only you can fix."

Zamora grilled the FBI liaison personnel about everything they had compiled about Anthony Montgomery, his in-laws, and the kidnapping. He, in turn, gave them what he could about Montgomery's involvement with the illegal steroid import and distribution business. Marciano looked thrilled. Zamora was sure that the young agent was feeling a rush of validation because his gut had been right about Montgomery. Marciano was probably anticipating his immediate advancement within the Bureau.

It was almost seven p.m. when Zamora finally got the go ahead to arrest Montgomery, and while he was in custody, get a sample of his DNA. As he accompanied Sanborn and Marciano to the Montgomery home, Zamora took a Cohiba cigar out of his right breast inside pocket, ran his tongue over the tip, then put in his mouth. He held it between his teeth but didn't light it. It was a four-hundred-dollar cigar, the purchase of which nearly caused his wife to divorce him. He had known, however, a time would come when his extravagance would be warranted, and that time was very soon. Actually smoking the Cohiba would be a commemorative luxury he would wait for. The bonus he would receive for his work on this case would certainly more than cover his self-indulgence.

When Montgomery was safely behind bars, Zamora would call Tia. He wondered what she would do to celebrate.

Jody and Tia were still on the foredeck. Their lovemaking had been so all-consuming that time had stood still for hours. They couldn't get enough of each other. Although at one point Tia wondered what was going on with the investigation, it was a fleeting thought that exited her head as quickly as it had entered. All she wanted to do was make love to the woman in her arms, again and again and again.

It was getting chilly, a cool breeze starting to build, but neither of them noticed it at first. Jody had spent the last fifteen minutes with her face buried in Tia's center, following her instincts and fulfilling Tia's desires. It was a wonderful realization that her own body had the capacity to respond in ways she'd never thought possible, but what *power* to know that she could coax such reactions out of another human being, that her sexual attentions could literally render them nearly helpless.

Jody rested her head on her hand and smugly watched Tia recover from what seemed to have been an earth-shattering climax. Tia's hand had a white-knuckle death grip on the bench cushion as her breath rasped in her throat.

"Jesus, Jody. I can't remember the last time anyone rocked my world like that."

"Not even Maria?"

When Tia remained silent, Jody thought she might have overstepped her boundaries by mentioning Tia's dead lover. She was about to apologize when Tia curled her fingers around Jody's.

"Yes, Maria did rock my world," she said softly. "But it was different. Maria tapped into my feral side, and she knew exactly what to do to feed it. You reach a much deeper part of me. When you make love with me, I feel it comes from your soul and not just your libido. As much as I loved Maria, couldn't resist her, she loved her husband and belonged to him. I may have given her what she needed in bed, but that's all I was to her."

"But didn't you tell me earlier that you would have given up your career for her?"

"Yeah. Silly, huh?" Tia sighed. "She would have kept me around, too. And I would have stayed, just to be near her, even knowing she didn't love me. She had that kind of a spell on me."

Jody listened, rapt. She was touched by the sad affection in Tia's voice as she spoke of the woman she loved. She waited for Tia's moment of melancholy to pass, and then she said, "I understand. That appears to be the kind of spell you have on me."

"If that's true, then I cast a spell that will last for all eternity." Tia waved her hand in the air as though she had actually bewitched their future.

Jody felt a warmth envelop her that seemed different from sexual heat. As quickly as it had materialized, it disappeared, and it was then that she became conscious of the cool current of air. "Let's adjourn to the master stateroom."

After another drink and some creative making out up against the wall, Jody found herself thrown on the bed. She lay on her back and looked up at Tia with a coquettishly nervous expression, her breathing labored by curiosity and excitement.

Tia joined Jody on the bed and said in a husky whisper, "Let's get adventurous."

Jody blanched. "You mean we haven't been?"

Tia grabbed Jody's ankles, turned her over, and pulled her up so Jody was on her hands and knees. Tia crouched between Jody's legs, spread her, and held her apart with her knees against Jody's thighs. She gathered an abundance of moisture from Jody's center and rimmed Jody's anus with her middle finger, then entered gradually and buried her finger deeper with each slow thrust. With her other hand, she fingered Jody to an almost violent orgasm that seemed to radiate from two areas at once.

"Oh Jesus, Tia. Oh my God, my God, please don't stop."

When Jody had recovered from her orgasm, Tia fucked her again in the same way. While Jody collapsed on the bed, Tia went to the head and washed her hands. She returned before Jody even knew she was gone. Tia turned Jody over onto her back "I am so going to make you mine," Tia muttered as she cupped Jody's breasts. She positioned herself over the neatly trimmed, reddish-blonde curls that sheltered Jody's sex, then blew on the dampness of the soft fringe. Tia parted Jody with her thumbs and proceeded to feast on Jody's aching center.

Jody felt as though she had died and gone to heaven. She could not, would not lose this woman.

Chapter 26

Anyone who angers you, conquers you.
—Elizabeth Kenny

Montgomery sighed as he settled into a chair in his lighted pool area. With the exception of a few minor glitches, everything had gone according to his plan. The FBI was scratching their collective heads; Bruce and Tia were trapped by their own addictions; and his poor wife was just a victim of circumstance. Tomorrow would be the last day of fun and games, and the next would be doomsday for his wife, Bruce, and that bitch, Ramone. His father-in-law was readying the ransom money, precisely what he'd thought would happen. He knew his father-in-law would cave and pay the money, and afterwards, he would be free of it all. *People are so predictable.* He laughed to himself. As for him, he would be so "grief-stricken" that he would appoint someone to run his company, and he would sell this house and move somewhere to mourn. Somewhere tropical, of course.

"Inez, could you get me another Seven and Seven?" Montgomery held out his glass to the downstairs maid. "Fresh glass, and easy on the ice this time."

"Yes, Mr. Montgomery." Inez took the glass. "Mr. Montgomery?"

"Yes, Inez?"

"May I ask, please, if there is any news on Mrs. Montgomery?"

"No, Inez, I'm sorry. The kidnappers still have her."

"We miss her very much, Mr. Montgomery. And Richard said a couple of the dogs aren't eating."

"Everything will be fine, Inez. The FBI is doing everything they can, and if all else fails, Mrs. Montgomery's father is willing to pay the ransom. She'll be home soon, I'm sure of it."

"Mr. Montgomery, forgive me, but Eeyore and Piglet are sleeping in my quarters at night," Inez said.

"That's okay. I'm sure Mrs. Montgomery would have wanted that, Inez. She knew how fond you were of that old dog and old cat."

Inez nodded. "Thank you, Mr. Montgomery." She went over to the wet bar on the patio to mix his cocktail.

Montgomery hoped Inez hadn't caught his referring to Jody in the past tense. At least for the next two days, he'd have to think before he spoke. As Inez handed him his drink, the houseman appeared.

"Mr. Montgomery? Agents Sanborn and Marciano are here to see you. May I show them out here?"

"Certainly, Richard." He took a sip of his drink and nodded at Inez. "Perfect. Thank you." Montgomery stood up, smoothed back his wet hair, and took a deep breath. Had something gone wrong? Had that maniac Ramone flipped out and killed Jody ahead of schedule? If that bitch had jumped the gun on him, he wouldn't get the payoff. Several scenarios ran through his mind, most of which centered around what he would do to Tia Ramone if she had fucked things up for him in any way. Montgomery plastered a fake smile on his face and faced the patio door as Richard led the agents outside. "Gentlemen, what can I do for you? Is there news about my wife?"

"No, sir, this is about you," Sanborn advised him.

They were joined by a tall man Montgomery had never seen. He looked to be of Hispanic descent. He had a different air about him, a streetwise authority that didn't set at all well with Montgomery. "Me?" He looked genuinely stunned. Bruce had assured him that everything incriminating had been removed from his computer, and even if the authorities did think there was more to find, Bruce had guaranteed that it would take a very long time to decipher it.

Could Bruce have set him up? No. Maybe Ramone might be insane enough to take things into her own hands, but Bruce wanted that payoff. Not only that, he was a follower, not a leader. "Did you have more questions? I honestly can't think of anything else I can tell you."

"We do have a question or two, sir. We need to know about your association with a woman named Roxanna Martindale," Walt Sanborn stated.

Montgomery feigned confusion. "I can't help you gentlemen. I am not personally acquainted with anyone by that name. I'm a happily married man. I don't associate with prostitutes."

"How do you know she's a prostitute, Mr. Montgomery?" Sanborn asked with a lift of his eyebrow.

"I heard about her on the news. It was the only other story making headlines the day the media stopped everything to report my wife's kidnapping. It was almost a relief to hear something other than the press speculating about my wife. So, of course I know the name. She was the hooker found dead in a car. I thought they were looking for some former CIA person in connection with that."

"Maybe you know her better as Roxi," Marciano suggested.

Montgomery swallowed hard and attempted to remain calm. "I told you, Agent Marciano, I don't associate with prostitutes. You've seen pictures of my wife. Why would I?"

Marciano's expression verged on being a smirk. "Mr. Montgomery, that's like a rapist saying, 'I can get any girl I want, why would I have to rape anyone?' You need to come clean with us, sir, and you need to do it now." His voice wasn't threatening, but it was firm.

"I don't like what you are implying," Montgomery said indignantly.

The DEA agent was less diplomatic than Marciano. He did smirk. "Then you'll like this even less."

Montgomery started to sweat, even while trying to pretend he was offended. "I'm sorry. You are?"

"Agent Zamora, DEA."

Montgomery paled. *Oh, no… no, no, no, no.* "The Drug Enforcement Administration? Why are you here?"

"I have a message for you from Tia Ramone: your little Scorpion has just stung you."

His face drained of its remaining color. "Ramone? I don't know who that is."

"Funny, you didn't know Roxanna Martindale, either, but you remembered her name from the news. Yet you don't remember Tia Ramone's name from the same broadcasts?" Marciano asked Montgomery.

"Oh… oh, wait, Ramone. That's the name of the CIA person who—"

"Save it." Zamora held up his hand. "What you will remember about Tia Ramone is that she's the one responsible for bringing you down. By the way, didn't anyone ever tell you not to underestimate a woman?"

Montgomery's eyes grew wide as three uniformed police officers appeared on the patio. Since he was dressed only in a Speedo water polo swimsuit, it was obvious he wasn't hiding anything and didn't need to be frisked. When he saw a pair of handcuffs being pulled from a woven leather holster, Montgomery took a step back. "Now wait a minute. Are you going to arrest me? What in the hell for?"

"Anthony Holt Montgomery, Junior, you are under arrest for conspiracy to import anabolic steroids, conspiracy to distribute anabolic steroids, conspiracy to launder money, and criminal forfeiture. You are also being arrested on suspicion of violating the Federal Kidnapping Act." Zamora purposely omitted the murder charge, as that was not his jurisdiction. That was a local police matter, and they had yet to match Montgomery's DNA with that of the unidentified spots in the car. Zamora had no doubt they would.

"What! This is insane! You can't..." Montgomery took several deep breaths to calm himself. "Okay. All right. Let me at least get dressed and call my lawyer."

The houseman suddenly stepped up next to Montgomery, a shirt and slacks slung over his outstretched arm. "Your clothes, sir."

Even though Montgomery continued to laugh incredulously, he was cooperative. He took his clothes and put them on over his bathing suit. "Richard, call my attorney, please. Have him meet me... Where? The FBI offices?"

"The police station, Harbor Precinct. We'll book you there and transport you following your arraignment," Sanborn said.

Montgomery looked at Marciano. "You're making a huge mistake. I didn't do anything, Danny. Don't fuck up your career over this. You're too young to go down in flames like this." Inside, Montgomery was imploding. *How could this have happened? How did that fucking bitch Ramone find out about the drugs?*

Marciano leaned in close and squinted at Montgomery. "Honestly, Mr. Montgomery, nothing could give me more pleasure than to do what I am doing right now."

Montgomery appeared to have regained his composure, but the beads of sweat above his lip contradicted his demeanor. "Dan, Dan, I'm telling you, this is a mistake."

"Tony, Tony," Marciano said, mocking him. "We have so much against you, you might never see the light of day again."

Montgomery instantly lost his nice guy persona; his face contorted in rage. "You stupid little son of a bitch! You are so going down for this. When my lawyer is finished with you, you won't be allowed to direct traffic."

Marciano leaned close to Montgomery's ear, so that only Montgomery could hear him. "Speaking of going down, a pretty boy like you is going to be very popular in federal prison. When we're finished with you, your asshole is going to pucker to the size of a pinpoint." Marciano smirked. "But don't worry, I'll send you a king sized jar of Vaseline. Where you're going, you'll need it." Marciano placed the handcuffs around Montgomery's wrists. "You have the right to remain silent..."

Jody couldn't speak for Tia, but she herself had been so thoroughly ravished, she was quite sure she wouldn't be able to walk comfortably for a while. The sex had been vigorous, to say the least, and she had enjoyed every second of it. No one had ever excited her as much as the woman in her arms, and Jody held Tia tightly in case this was the last time they would be able to be together for a while. She wondered what was going on with the investigation, wondered whether she would be home tomorrow, wondered whether Tia would be taken away from her, or worse, if Tia would leave on her own. She dozed off not long after Tia had started to snore lightly.

When Tia woke up to use the head, she checked her phone for messages. "Tia," Zamora's message said, on her voice mail, "it's over. We've got him. Stick that proverbial fork in him. He's done. I'm coming out there to get you two. We're bringing you home."

Zamora's message caused her to forget about her full bladder. His announcement had been left about twenty minutes earlier. "Shit." She rubbed the sleep out of her eyes with a sense of relief she hadn't felt in a long time and knelt by Jody's side of the bed. "Hey." She shook Jody gently, her voice soft so as not to startle her lover. "Jody, wake up."

Jody stretched languidly then winced. "Owwwww. Ooooh." She focused on Tia's smiling face. "Need more sleep... and a chiropractor," she mumbled.

"There'll be plenty of time for that. Tony's been arrested, and Javier and the feds are on their way here."

"They have him?" Jody sat up quickly and immediately regretted it. "Damn. I thought I was in shape." She rubbed her lower back.

Tia leaned over and kissed her. "Oh, you are. Trust me on that." She winked and stood up. "They should be here any minute. I'm going to the room I was sleeping in and mess it up to make it look like I spent the night there. I'm also going to shower." Her lips pursed into a smirk. "I suggest you do the same. And maybe strip the bed and throw the sheets into the washer. We don't need any appearance of witness tampering to cloud the issue. I'll be back to help you remake the bed."

Jody got out of the berth and began to pull off the bedding. "Tia?"

"Yes?"

"What happens now?"

"You'll be debriefed by the FBI and then—"

"No." She reached for Tia's wrist. "I mean between us."

"I… I don't know, Jody. That will be up to you. I have a lot of demons I need to exorcise before I do anything. I'm not whole right now, and you deserve someone who is. These are extraordinary circumstances. Under normal conditions, we might not even like each other." Tia's bearing was suddenly uncharacteristically vulnerable, as though she was giving Jody an excuse to pull away.

Jody smiled fondly. "I doubt that."

"Really?"

"Really." Jody squeezed Tia's hand.

Tia leaned over and tenderly kissed Jody. She hoped it wasn't for the last time.

Chapter 27

Nobody can go back and start a new beginning, but anyone can start today and make a new ending.
—Maria Anderson

It turned into a media frenzy. The local police department's Public Information Officer had contacted the press, and suddenly helicopters were everywhere. Spotlights illuminated *The Quintessence* as the federal agents boarded, disappeared inside, and returned with the missing heiress. Tia followed, Javier at her side.

The rescue was broadcast live all over the world, as was the news that Jody's husband had been arrested. He was suspected of being connected to the abduction, along with other serious charges. As Tia and Javier stepped onto the federal water transport, Zamora leaned in to Tia. "Damn, woman, you're still a ladykiller, aren't you?"

Tia tried to look innocent, but she knew exactly what he meant. "What are you talking about?"

"Jefa, you can take as many showers as you want, you can wash those sheets a thousand times, you can spray all the room freshener in there that the manufacturers have to offer, but that room still smells like sex." He waggled his eyebrows.

A faint blush colored her cheeks. "Shut up, Javi. You always did have an extra-sensitive nose."

Zamora threw his head back and let go a hearty laugh. "Perro." He gestured Tia to the lower deck and the waiting boat.

Tia seated herself opposite Jody, who was flanked by two FBI agents. Their eyes met and locked, communicating so much more than words ever could. If their interaction was detected, no one made mention of it. The agents were speaking to Jody Montgomery the entire thirty-minute journey back to shore. Tia couldn't hear what they were saying, but she saw Jody either nod or shake her head in response to their questions.

Once they docked, cameras and microphones were shoved into their faces, and questions, insinuations, and accusations were thrown at them from every direction. Until they were each safely ensconced in separate SUVs, the only words spoken were, "No comment."

The Wainwrights watched the entire event unfold on live TV. Staff, acquaintances, and law enforcement officials all offered their congratulations to Jody's parents. John almost bawled like a baby when he saw his daughter emerge onto the aft deck landing, where she was courteously assisted onto the government vessel. She looked tired.

Sondra remained phlegmatic but was appalled to find herself choking up, something she would never acknowledge or admit to anyone. They had already been informed that Montgomery had been arrested. Sondra had scoffed at John's shock, but she herself was also surprised that her son-in-law had risked so much. Both she and John assumed it had been about the ransom money and for no other reason. Sondra understood revenge, but only if it had dollar signs attached to it.

They didn't speak to one another as they remained glued to the news networks, listening intently to each reporter speculate about what had happened, what was currently happening, and what would most likely happen in the immediate future. Everyone present on the Wainwright estate watched the huge television screen in silence as film of Jody being escorted into the regional FBI headquarters was intercut with snippets of Montgomery, in shackles, being led into the Harbor police station.

Several hours later, tired of interrogation but happy to be free, Jody was escorted to her parents' home by federal security agents. Her reunion with her father was tearful, sweet, and precious. She knew how deeply and sincerely her father loved her. "Daddy, I'm fine," she assured him. "Officer Ramone was very protective. I was very, very lucky to have had her in the right place at the right time. If it weren't for her, I would be dead." The finality of that last word made them both cry. When Jody eventually regained control, she drew away from her father and went to her mother.

Her reunion with her mother was altogether different. She hugged her mother for the cameras, her lips very close to Sondra's ear. For the first time she addressed her mother in a way she'd never previously had the guts to. "You cold, insufferable bitch. I watched you on the news. You couldn't have cared less if I returned safely. Don't worry... I won't lay a straw in your way, but if you think, for one minute, I'm going to continue to tolerate your insecurities in regards to me, you can think again. Get your shit together, Mother. I'm warning you. I'm not the little girl who was under your thumb a few days ago."

There was an authority in Jody's voice that did not brook argument. Sondra tightened her grip on Jody. "After all of this..." Her voice broke. "I know I haven't been the best mother, but I'm so glad, so very glad you weren't hurt. Please believe that, Jody."

Jody swallowed hard and slowly pushed back from Sondra. "I wish I could believe that." She turned to face the cameras. "I'm very grateful to be home. That's all I have to say for now." And, with that, Jody, John, and Sondra walked arm-in-arm into John's private study, where there was no press. A cordon of police officers prevented anyone from following them.

A short while later, Jody returned to her own home. After basking in the sincere, warm welcome from her staff, Jody checked on all of her animals, thanking everyone who had helped keep them fed, exercised, and healthy.

That evening, Jody took a relaxing swim with her lab/beagle mix, Piglet, who attempted to swim laps with her. Eeyore, her gray Maltese cat, supervised intently. When she finally went to bed, her faithful companions snuggled in with her, but Jody keenly felt Tia's absence.

Bruce recounted his testimony to a delegation of DEA supervisors and deal makers. They were already in possession of Bruce's CDs, and what he told them in his deposition supported the recordings. Some personnel were annoyed that someone complicit in the kidnapping had been promised immunity, but others knew Bruce was the small fish in the Big Pond who was helping them catch a Big Fish. When his taped testimony for the preliminary hearing was completed, he was snapped up into witness protection and relocated to Wyoming.

Twenty miles away, in a secure location arranged by Javier, Tia sipped on a club soda. She'd been raked over the coals by the FBI. It took hours to satisfy them that she hadn't been working with Montgomery, that she had been working with Bruce Wechsler and

Javier Zamora to bring Montgomery down. She explained how Montgomery had solicited her and Bruce separately, but that they had both realized the only way they could bring him down was to work together. What she told them was compelling, and her story was not only backed up by Wechsler, it was supported by Jody Montgomery, as well. No matter how many ways they tried to trip her up, her story didn't vary.

Now she was watching herself on the news, with the sound muted, and missing Jody. As though a piece of her had been forever lost, the emptiness she felt was almost unbearable. She settled in, propped herself against the headboard, and began to flip through channels. She took another swallow of club soda. Her head was amazingly clear. She hadn't had a drop of alcohol in more than twenty-four hours. That was a record. The CIA had contacted her to praise her for her actions and apologize for theirs. That was one thing. But it was quite another when they told her they would expunge the blots on her service record and asked her to come back to work. After she told them in no uncertain terms to do something anatomically impossible with their offer, mixed with the events of the last few days, her conscience felt better than it had in a long time.

Montgomery sat in jail, awaiting transport to a federal facility. *How could everything have gone so wrong? I had everything under control. And now...* The evidence against him was pretty damned overwhelming. He must have vastly underestimated Tia Ramone and her powers of persuasion, especially on his wife.

Jody. He should have been happy that his wife wasn't dead. After all, she had only been a pawn in his plan for revenge. But he wasn't happy at all. He felt a fury raging inside him beyond anything he had ever experienced. Ramone had used his wife's innocence and vulnerability against him. His own wife should have believed him, but she hadn't. She had turned against him in the blink of an eye. He couldn't believe she had been so ready to sell him out on the word of Bruce and Ramone. They were degenerates, and yet she had sided with them. And to make matters even worse, Jody was still alive, which meant Wainwright wasn't suffering.

When he was informed that Jody was there and requesting to visit him, he was stunned.

Jody sat in a visiting room that was normally reserved for lawyer/client meetings. She was on one side of a narrow, dented metal table, all that would separate her from her soon-to-be ex-husband. Tony was a celebrity at the minimum-security facility where he was currently being held, but he was about to be transferred into federal custody. Guards were everywhere. She could feel their eyes on her, even though they were trying to be discreet.

Agent Zamora had reminded Jody to be careful what she said to her husband, because everything was monitored and recorded. She had been prepped by Zamora, who wondered out loud why Jody felt the need to meet with Montgomery at all. It was hard for Jody to explain, other than she felt they had unfinished business.

Jody heard the screech of a metal bolt sliding, and she looked up to see Tony standing in the sallyport, dressed in prison orange scrubs, his hands shackled to the chain around his waist. When the exterior door was secured, the officer escorting Tony requested the opening of the door to the visitor room. Jody heard the lock being electronically released, and the officer pushed the inner door open and escorted Tony inside. The guard helped Tony into the chair opposite Jody then stepped back and stood against the wall, directly across from the visiting room's stationary officer.

Jody clenched her teeth and restrained herself from slapping Tony across the face. It was she who finally broke the uncomfortable silence. "You look like hell."

"Really? Imagine that. This place is just like Club Med. I'll have to speak to the management."

"I won't ask you why, Tony. From everything I've been told and everything I've read, it's clear to me why you did all of the horrible things you did. I just need to know—did I ever mean anything to you?"

"Why is that important now? You believed that bitch. You protected her."

"You can't be serious. You were going to kill me."

"According to that drunk, lying piece of burnt out shit and that drugged up geek."

"I heard you with my own ears, Tony."

"Did you? Are you sure? Or was it the geek doing his computer thing with voices?"

"How would he know about your 'scorpion' nickname for me?"

"I have no idea. They set me up, Jody. I find it amazing that you would side with people you say you didn't even meet until they kidnapped you, that you would believe them over your husband. For all I know, you were in it with them. Maybe you told them about my nickname for you."

She stared at him, mouth agape. "Oh my God, you are really something. We both know the truth here."

He leaned closer, his sneer challenging. "Yes, we do, don't we?"

She didn't rise to his baiting. She drew a deep breath and exhaled. "Yes, we do. And it will all come out during the trial. If your credibility and character weren't in question, if they didn't have concrete evidence against you, you wouldn't be here, would you? Ms. Ramone and Mr. Wechsler would be here instead of you, wouldn't they?" She met his glare with one of her own.

"Why are you here?" His voice held undisguised resentment, his attitude one of indignation. "You want me to say I'm sorry? Don't hold your breath. I didn't do anything wrong. If I'm sorry about anything, it's that you betrayed me."

"I betrayed *you?"* Jody studied him. "I don't know you anymore. What happened to you?"

"Nothing. I'm the same man I always was." Montgomery sat back.

"If that's true, how horribly sad for you. For both of us, actually."

His rigid expression and posture told her their conversation was over. He shoved the chair back and stood up. "Officer, can you take me back to my cell, please."

Chapter 28

Love is an unusual game. There are either two winners or none.
                                                    —Anonymous

One week after Montgomery's transfer to federal custody, Tia emerged from one-hundred-and-twenty-eight hours of concentrated rehabilitation. She was feeling a little lost in her sobriety, but clear-headed. The first person she contacted was Joanne Dyson Wainwright Montgomery. They'd had no contact with one another since the rescue. Now that Jody had had some time to herself in which to consider their relationship, Tia needed to know where she stood. When Jody accepted her call instantly, seemingly without reservation, Tia's heart flooded with emotion.

"Oh Lord, Tia, you have no idea how much I've missed you," Jody breathed into the phone She sounded ecstatic.

Tia grinned, pleased that Jody sounded sincerely happy to hear from her. "I think I might have some idea."

"When am I going to see you?"

"How about sometime between yesterday and tomorrow?"

"Please," Jody said, "come now."

"As much as I would love to, I think we need to consider your reputation."

"Fuck my reputation."

Tia smiled. "It's not your reputation I'm interested in fucking. Where are you?"

"*The Quintessence*. I had to get away from everything. I know it must sound silly, but being here makes me feel closer to you."

"No," Tia said warmly. "It doesn't sound silly at all. I'm surprised *The Quintessence* isn't still impounded as evidence."

"They released it to me yesterday and—"

"Is your security person back on board?"

"Kevin? No. Kevin fell and broke his leg on his climb up Everest. Poor guy never made it to the summit. He'll be laid up for a while. I actually had an advanced security system installed. There are sensors everywhere that will alert me if any object larger than a seal comes within a thousand feet of the yacht. My father insisted that I hire armed bodyguards to be with me. He said a security system is pretty useless if there's no one around to respond to it, but then that would kind of negate the 'getting away' part, you know?"

"So, did you resolve that?"

"I rented the security guys a nice little boat of their own so they can keep an eye on me from a distance. If any person or object penetrates the perimeter, security is automatically notified and can check it out immediately. My guess would be that until they hear that alarm go off, they'll be relaxing and taking advantage of a big screen TV in their salon." Jody sighed in anticipation. "I can disarm the system until you get on board, but the press is still all around here."

"Unless I can come up with a plan, we may have to wait."

"The thought of one more day without you in my arms is torture."

Tia smiled. "You can't always get what you want when you want it, you know," she teased.

"Somehow I doubt that would be true if I had you here," Jody teased back.

The media horde that had flooded around the yacht following Jody's rescue had diminished to a trickle when the story was no longer fresh. A few members of the press had lingered near Jody, just in case any new angle became available. Now that she had retrieved *The Quintessence* and taken it back out, there was more activity surrounding the yacht again. It would have been the perfect place to reunite with Tia, but Jody was concerned about the reunion turning into a salacious circus if reporters discovered Tia was there with her. Even so, she had neither the strength nor the desire to tell Tia to wait for a more appropriate time. There might never be a more appropriate time.

Tia seemed to have more restraint, maybe because of her CIA training. Knowing she was so close and yet seemed so far away, frustrated and depressed Jody. She could take the yacht in and meet Tia somewhere, but there would be no way she could do that without having the media all over it.

She was startled from her pity party by the beeping of the alarm that indicated a malfunction. Her phone rang immediately; the guards were on the ball. As she answered the call, Jody went to the alarm panel in the salon and found that the activation light was blinking. "Yes?"

"Mrs. Montgomery, this is Phillip. Looks like we've got a trouble signal on your alarm."

"Yes. I'm looking at the panel now."

"We're on our way. Stay on the phone with me until we get there. Go back into the master stateroom and lock yourself in until we've checked everything out. Does your panel indicate what area originated the signal?"

"I can't pinpoint the source of the problem, but I thought a trouble signal just meant a malfunction," Jody said.

"It usually does, but we don't want to take the chance that you might be in danger."

When Jody walked into the master stateroom, she gasped at seeing there was now another person on the yacht with her.

"Mrs. Montgomery? What's wrong?" Phillip asked.

Jody couldn't believe her lover was in front of her, naked and toweling off. Surprised blue eyes took in the seductive grin and immediately misted over. "Stop, don't come! Uh... everything's fine. I see the problem. Let me try to fix it," Jody said into the phone.

"Mrs. Montgomery, you know the code words. If you're in danger, say it, if you are not, say it."

"Eeyore," Jody said. That was the password she had chosen to advise them everything was fine. "Listen, I'm resetting it right now. If that doesn't work, I always have my little panic button."

"Are you sure you don't want us to at least do a perimeter check and walk-through?"

"I'm positive. Thanks. I'll call you back if the reset doesn't work." She snapped her phone shut and flew into Tia's arms, sobbing. "I am so happy to see you."

"Shhhh, shhhh, it's okay, baby." Tia squeezed Jody to her, swaying them back and forth. "I'm happy to see you, too." She kissed the top of Jody's head. "Let's reactivate that alarm system before we have visitors." She watched as Jody pressed a six-digit combination on the panel. A beep sounded and the "perimeter ready" green light changed to the "perimeter armed" red light. Tia turned Jody around to face her and stepped backward, slowly drawing Jody to the berth. They fell back onto the cushioned softness of the bedcovers and began to kiss feverishly. Tia rolled over onto Jody as Jody buried her hands in Tia's damp hair.

"How did you do that?" Jody asked between delicious kisses.

"Does it matter?"

"Absolutely not, but tell me anyway." Jody sighed contently as Tia nuzzled her neck.

"I'm a certified diver, and I've been trained to use my skills covertly," Tia mumbled against Jody's skin.

"But the alarm went off when you were already on board. It should have sounded the second you hit the perimeter."

Tia propped herself up on one elbow and slid her hand under Jody's tank top. "The body temperature of fish is the same as the temperature of the water they're in. That's why they don't set off your alarm, which is set up to alert on a warm-blooded form. I have a few tools left over from The Agency. One I brought with me can neutralize small-scale laser and infrared beams. That's what caused it to read as a trouble signal rather than an intrusion."

"Soooo talented," Jody drawled, then closed her eyes as Tia's hand cupped her breast. "Mmmm..."

They kissed passionately, and Jody fit her bare thigh between Tia's long legs, feeling heat and wetness there. They made out a while longer then took a break to catch their breath. Jody stared at Tia reverently as Tia gently traced Jody's facial features with trembling fingers.

Jody's expression of awe stopped Tia's caress. "What?" Tia asked.

"I fell in love with you the minute I saw you, you know," Jody told her.

"I know." Tia smirked and received a sharp yank on her hair in retaliation.

"Aren't we just the cocky one?" Jody teased.

Tia turned her head and kissed the inside of Jody's wrist several times until Jody eased her grip. "Come on, you like 'em dangerous and you like it rough, but because of who you are, you have to be clandestine about it. I don't have to be cocky to know I'm the woman for you." Tia lowered her face to Jody's, kissed her, and started pressing against her thigh.

"Tia, let me get undressed—"

"No." Tia's focus was on her inflamed center as she rocked on Jody's upper leg. "Should have worn your robe," she said, panting.

Jody began to move in tandem with Tia's rhythm. "Oh Jesus, Tia, please..."

"Please what?" Tia pressed her body snugly to Jody's and pushed her thigh into Jody's center, eliciting a sharp gasp. "Please *what?*" Tia forcefully whispered in her ear. She increased her momentum, grinding harder as she felt Jody latch on.

"Oh God, Tia, please fuck me, please fuck me right now!"

Chapter 29

Love me when I least deserve it, because that's when I really need it.
—Swedish Proverb

Jody was invited to do exclusive interviews with Oprah Winfrey, Larry King, and Barbara Walters, among others, but she politely declined all offers. The weekly news and entertainment magazines also vied in bidding wars to get a print interview with her, but she wasn't interested. She just wanted to move on, but Tia advised her that she needed to give the media something, otherwise she would never get any peace. *They* would never get any peace.

Jody finally gave in. She met with her father's legal team and law enforcement representatives and arranged a press conference. Jody was prepared, and she wasn't. She had been dealing with the media all her life, but never had any press conference been concentrated on her at such a personal level. Typically any publicity she dealt with had to do with her pedigree or her charities.

As Tia waited in another room and watched the pandemonium unfold on the TV monitors, she openly admired the aplomb with which Jody handled the media. With a cadre of family attorneys at her side, she walked out and sat behind a long desk equipped with a microphone. She was facing national and international news and television reporters, hoping the press would buy into everything she was about to tell them.

Agent Danny Marciano handled the introductions, and after a brief statement from the DEA's Public Information Officer, the floor was opened to the media.

"Mrs. Montgomery, how are you doing?"

Jody recognized the young male reporter from the network news. "I'm fine, considering. Thank you for asking." Jody was gracious and charming.

"Mrs. Montgomery, can you tell us how you came to meet Tia Ramone?" the same reporter asked, slipping another question through before any of the others.

Jody smiled. This was a question they had specifically prepared for. "Yes. I was contacted by Ms. Ramone on the evening of September thirteenth. She advised me of my husband's plans to have me abducted, held for ransom, and then murdered."

"What made you believe her?" another perfectly coiffed, well-modulated reporter inquired.

"Honestly, I didn't believe her, at first. She advised me that on the following night, September fourteenth, my husband would take me out to dinner at The Cypress, which he did, and he would drug my glass of wine, which he did. She further advised me that he had planned out my route and knew I would feel the effects of the drug somewhere near the Dillon rest stop on Dillon Highway and that I would pull over at that location. Which I did."

"You drank the wine, even though you had been told it was drugged?"

"Yes. I initially thought Ms. Ramone's knowledge of my dinner date with my husband could have been something she overheard. I drank a glass of wine with dinner, as I usually do. When I began to get sleepy approaching the Dillon rest stop, I knew Ms. Ramone was telling the truth. Before I passed out, Ms. Ramone met me at the rest stop and I willingly agreed to accompany her to my yacht until I had a clear head and we could figure things out."

"How did he know you would take Dillon Highway?"

"Because that's the most direct route from The Cypress to our house. I had taken it many times in the past."

"Mrs. Montgomery, how did you know you could trust Tia Ramone?"

"Given the situation in which I found myself, I didn't have much of a choice."

"Mrs. Montgomery, why didn't you at least contact your parents and tell them that you were okay?"

"The DEA agent working the case advised me to stay silent until they could build a solid case against my husband. He said it would be safer for everyone involved if Tony wasn't tipped off, even inadvertently."

"Would that DEA person be Agent Zamora?"

"Yes."

"Mrs. Montgomery, how did Agent Zamora get involved?"

"When Ms. Ramone uncovered information about my husband's, um, other activities, she immediately contacted Agent Zamora and provided him with information. From that point on, we deferred to Agent Zamora's expertise and direction."

"When did Agent Zamora contact the FBI to advise them you were alive and well?"

"That's a question you would have to ask Agent Zamora."

"Have you had contact with your husband since his arrest?"

"Yes. I went to see him before he was transferred into federal custody."

"Would you like to expound on that meeting for us?"

Jody smiled politely but said firmly, "I would not."

"Mr. Montgomery's defense is that he was set up. Any comment on that?"

"I think the evidence will speak for itself. Since his case is pending, I can't go into any specifics at this time."

"Are you going to maintain an association with Tia Ramone?"

"Absolutely. I have hired her as my personal security consultant. She will be accompanying me everywhere. After the events of the last two weeks, I'll feel much safer with her presence."

"Mrs. Montgomery, there's a rumor that you and Ms. Ramone got rather, uh, close during this ordeal. Care to elaborate on that?"

Jody—and everyone else in the room—knew what the reporter was asking. Jody tried to defuse the innuendo. "Ms. Ramone saved my life while putting her own at risk. She had to guard me 24/7 until this case was concluded. No one was on that yacht except Ms. Ramone and myself, so, yes, I would say that would qualify as getting close."

"Your husband's statement claims that you and Ms. Ramone became lovers. Is that true?"

"What paper did you say you were with? *The Enquirer?*" That got a laugh from the crowd of reporters. "My husband will say anything to take the onus off of himself. If he wants to put his little fantasy on the record, hoping it might make him look less guilty, more power to him."

"You didn't answer the question, Mrs. Montgomery," the reporter persisted.

Jody leveled him with a cool gaze. "I believe I did." She pointed to a female on the other side of the room. "Next question."

"Do you know why your husband thought Ms. Ramone was going along with his plan?"

"If you're looking for a specific answer, that's something you'll have to ask him. I do know that Ms. Ramone told me he approached her after the person he first approached refused to kidnap and murder me. That witness then provided my husband with Ms. Ramone's name, and that's when my husband trapped her—" She heard a lawyer behind her clear his throat. "Excuse me, I mean *allegedly* trapped her into assisting with his plans."

"How did the anonymous witness know of Ms. Ramone?"

"From what I understand, he had heard her name through a relative. I don't know any more than that."

"Mrs. Montgomery." The tabloid reporter spoke up again, drawing annoyed looks from his competition. "Tia Ramone has admitted she was in a vehicle with a now-deceased prostitute for the sole purpose of having sex, and that's where the initial meeting with your husband took place. How do you feel about that?"

"I feel that is none of my business." But the idea of it did gnaw at her. The thought of Tia with anyone else bothered her.

"Mrs. Montgomery, will you expedite your divorce proceedings?"

"If I can find a legal means, absolutely."

"Is that so you can be with Tia Ramone?" the rag magazine reporter asked obstinately.

Jody took a deep breath and plastered on her most patient smile. She had to choose her words carefully. The last thing she wanted to do was jeopardize the case against Tony. He could still be freed on some idiotic technicality. She knew what she wanted to say, but a tirade would make her look naive and foolish. Well ... *more* naive and foolish than Tony had already made her look.

"You heard the list of federal charges against my husband. The kidnapping, solicitation, and conspiracy charges had to do with me. The evidence and witness statements allege that he wanted me murdered. And you think I want to divorce him so I can be with someone else?" There was dead silence in the room as she stared down the reporter. "Are there any other legitimate questions?"

The tabloid reporter didn't even have the decency to look embarrassed. He smirked and scribbled something in his pocket notebook.

A female correspondent pulled Jody's focus away from the tabloid reporter. "Mrs. Montgomery, are you saying you had no idea your husband was involved in the alleged drug activity?"

"Absolutely none. Tony and I were married, yes, but we had different interests and basically led separate lives."

"Are you saying you had a marriage in name only?" It was Mr. RagMag again.

"No. We were married in every sense of the word. What I am saying is the man sitting in federal custody right now is not the man I thought I was married to." This reporter was really getting on her nerves. When he attempted to jump in with another question, Jody ignored him.

This happened two more times before the reporter shouted over everyone, "Mrs. Montgomery, why don't you want to answer my questions?"

"I am answering your questions, sir, as ridiculously lurid as they are. But we have limited time here, and I think you should give your colleagues a chance to—"

"I am pursuing a legitimate story, regardless of how uncomfortable it might be for you. A good reporter needs to speak up to be heard."

"And needs to shut up to be appreciated. I don't have to be here. I'm granting this press conference, which means I can just as easily thank you all for coming and say goodbye, which would leave you to face your peers who didn't get to ask their questions. I'm done talking to you. I'm not answering any more intimate questions. That is not up for discussion."

Tia grinned at the monitor. She admired the way Jody never lost her temper, not once. By now, Tia would have knocked out all his teeth and pounded him into the ground. The way Jody confidently took command of the room was just plain hot. This was the public side of her lover, a side Jody had been groomed for since birth, a side with which Tia was unfamiliar. A side that made Tia want to whisk Jody out of the conference hall and back to *The Quintessence*.

When the inquisition was over and Jody, followed by an obligatory entourage of officialdom, returned to the back room where Tia waited for her, Tia was leaning casually against the wall. Eyes twinkling, arms crossed, she smiled at Jody and mouthed, "I love you."

Jody nodded slightly, grinned confidently, and mouthed back, "I know."

Tia's heart lurched as realization hit her full force. She hadn't saved Jody's life. Jody had saved hers.

Epilogue

True love doesn't consist of holding hands— it consists of holding hearts.
   —Anonymous

John and Sondra were invited onto *The Quintessence* for a quiet dinner during which Jody and Tia were going to make an announcement. It was one of the many gestures the younger couple had made Jody's parents to help them get comfortable with their marriage. The relationship between Jody and her mother was beginning to smooth out but could still turn prickly at any given moment. Jody wanted to believe that Sondra was honest in her words and actions, but after so many years of her mother's disrespect and dismissive treatment, she found it hard to trust Sondra's sincerity.

"I think she's made a determined effort to change her attitude toward you," Tia said to Jody as they made sure everything was ready for the visit. "She's doing her best to spend quality time with you, and since you and I have settled in, she's stopped seeing you as competition. Not only has that made her tolerable, it's made her almost pleasant to be around, and that beats the hell out of her being so icy and detached." Tia stopped and thought about her words. "Now she's almost annoyingly hospitable and exasperatingly solicitous."

"I agree… to a point. But, come on, Daddy has certainly given her the incentive to behave herself."

"You mean threatening her with divorce if she doesn't toe the line?" Tia chuckled. "How many times do you think he can use that before it loses its potency?"

"Enough times for it to work." Jody smiled and pulled Tia into an embrace. "Plus, mother doesn't want to cross you. You effectively scare the nastiness right out of her... at least to our faces."

Tia's arms circled Jody's shoulders. "Nah, she just likes me better than you." Tia lowered her head to capture a quick kiss from her wife. She received a peck on the lips and a swat on her behind.

"She probably does." Jody had a hint of sting in her tone.

Tia tightened her hold. "Then she's a bigger fool than I originally thought." She kissed her again, this one more lingering.

"Don't get me all hot and bothered before they get here, you know my hormones are already out of control," Jody lovingly admonished after she broke a kiss that had quickly gone from routine to passionate.

Tia looked at her watch. "They shouldn't be here for another fifteen minutes. I could—"

A hand clamped over Tia's mouth. "Shush. I don't want to hear it. It would be our luck that they'd get here early." She removed her hand. "And fifteen minutes would never be enough time to—"

Tia placed her hand over Jody's mouth. "I thought you didn't want to hear it," Tia teased. She moved her hand and replaced it with her lips.

After another heated kiss, Jody broke away, her breathing beginning to be labored. "What were we talking about?"

"Your mother." Tia loved that she could so easily distract her wife.

Jody tucked her head under Tia's chin. "Right. Her." She moved out of Tia's embrace. "She's terrified of you," Jody said, a hint of relish in her voice.

"I don't know why. I've never uttered so much as a cross word to her."

"You don't have to. When she knows she's coming close to stepping over a line, there's a look you get on your face that stops her dead in her tracks."

"You mean this look?" Tia demonstrated the exact expression to which Jody referred.

"Yes, that one. Don't ever give me that look for real, okay? It's hilarious when you do it to Mother, but I never want to see it directed at me."

"It's good to know I have one defense you haven't penetrated yet," Tia said, amused. "I know you don't completely buy your mother's metamorphosis, but I'm glad you've stuck to your attempts to live in the present and not dwell on the past." She followed Jody to the salon. "How do you think they're going to take the news?"

"I think it will finally convince them I'm not going through a phase," Jody said, and smiled brightly. She ran her hand over her still flat belly. "I'm glad we're going to tell them before I start to show."

"Good Lord, that was delicious," John Wainwright said as he pushed his chair away from the table. He looked up at Tia, who was clearing the table. "So we can add gourmet cook to your many talents."

"Thank you, John, but no talent to it. You just make sure the artichokes are pre-cooked and add them to the capers, garlic, lemon juice, and olive oil, and pan sear the Ahi." Tia picked up the wine bottle and held it over his glass. "More?"

"Yes, that would be lovely." He cleared his throat as Tia poured. "Does it bother you when your guests drink in front of you?"

"John!" Sondra said, clearly embarrassed by her husband's question.

Tia smiled at her in-laws. "No. I really was never a fan of wine, so I have no craving to join you. Beer and scotch, on the other hand, I do miss. But I feel so much better not having alcohol in my system, that it's worth the fight to stay away from it."

"You're a strong woman, Tia," Sondra said. She looked over at Jody, who was beaming proudly at her wife. "Why aren't you having a glass of wine with us? You haven't given it up, have you?"

Jody and Tia exchanged glances. Tia nodded, as if to say, "Now is as good a time as any."

"Not permanently, no. Just for the next seven months or so." She waited for a reaction from her parents, but they stared at her blankly.

Finally John said, "I don't understand."

Tia walked around the table, stood behind Jody's chair, and placed her hands on Jody's shoulders. Jody looked up at her and back at her parents. "We didn't want to say anything until we were positive, but I've been trying to get pregnant, in vitro fertilization. I'm pregnant."

The only thing that changed about John and Sondra's expressions was that they seemed more perplexed.

"You can add that to my many talents if you'd like," Tia added dryly.

Sondra choked on her wine. John handed her a napkin to cover her mouth, in case she spewed.

"Are you okay, Mother?" Jody asked.

Her mother nodded and coughed as her father's face split into an excited grin. "An heir? Finally? You're going to have a child?"

"Yes," Jody confirmed as Tia squeezed her shoulders.

"But... how? When?"

"We've been trying for the last six months," Tia said. "It finally took two months ago."

"We went to a specialist. We really weren't expecting good news for at least another year, but I got lucky," Jody said.

John rose from his chair, and in two steps, he had Tia trapped in a bear hug. He pulled Jody to her feet and into the embrace. "This is wonderful news! Wonderful!" He looked over at Sondra, who had tears in her eyes and a hint of a smile on her face.

"I'm going to be a grandmother?" Sondra finally said.

"Yes, Mother." Jody was prepared for the pleased veneer Sondra had been wearing to crumble and fall to the floor. "I know how you feel, and don't worry, I won't ask you to babysit."

Before Sondra could respond, John said, "Well, you'd damned well better ask me."

Sondra stood and joined the group hug. "I'm thrilled for you both. Really." When they broke apart, Sondra added, "But I'm glad you won't ask me to babysit. You, of all people, Jody, know that children are not my forte." It was said without malice and Sondra's tone reflected a truth in her delight.

"Who's the father?" John asked, as everyone returned to their seats.

"Remember Agent Zamora?" Jody asked.

"I'll never forget him. He brought you home. He's the father?"

"We wanted the baby to share Tia's heritage, and we asked Javier to be the sperm donor."

"Isn't he married with a family?" Sondra asked.

"Yes, but it won't be a problem. He has waived all parental rights, and he's even offered to help us out again if we decide to give this one"—Jody patted her stomach—"a little brother or sister."

Tia saw that both John and Sondra were mentally reconciling the idea of having a half-Hispanic grandchild.

"Is there a problem?" Jody asked before Tia could.

John snapped out of his introspection. "No. No, not at all."

Two sets of eyes locked on Sondra. "No. He's a handsome man, so I have no doubt the baby will be attractive," Sondra said, her tone conciliatory. "Have you thought about names?"

"It's too soon. But he or she will have the last name of Wainwright," Jody said. When the divorce from Montgomery was final, Jody had gone to court and legally resumed her maiden name, openly declaring her love for Tia soon afterward. It had caused another media feeding frenzy, with scandalous speculation about possible impropriety in connection with the abduction.

The high-powered, highly paid Wainwright family attorneys put that rumor to rest by reissuing statements containing the indisputable evidence the government had used to convict Montgomery. Still, every once in a while, Tia and Jody became the tabloid story du jour, not that it made one bit of difference in their lives or with the Wainwright business contracts and arrangements. Even the most conservative or prejudiced businessperson transacting with John or Jody knew where his or her bread was buttered. When it came to dealing with the Wainwrights, they found a way to put their biases aside. If they wanted to stay successful, hate and prejudice were luxuries the clients couldn't afford.

"When can we make the formal announcement?" John asked. "I can't wait to tell those boardroom boys I'm going to have an heir."

"Yes. They were so smug when they heard the news that you were... well, not in a situation to give your father grandchildren, knowing how badly he wanted them," Sondra said.

"It's amazing the things you rich people get competitive about," Tia said.

"No argument there," John acknowledged. "So... when?"

Jody and Tia exchanged amused glances, and Jody looked at her father. "Not just yet. We'd like to wait until I start to show. We'd kind of like to have that first baby bump moment to ourselves."

John looked as though he would burst. "You have made me the happiest man alive."

John and Sondra were topside, waiting for their personal water taxi to take them back to shore. Tia was supposed to be below with Jody, who had a sudden bout of nausea, but she had settled Jody in the master berth and was on her way back upstairs when she overheard her in-laws in conversation.

"At least you're not hitting the roof like you did when they told us what was really going on between them," Sondra said.

"That's true. But it's not like we didn't suspect they had become close. I thought Jody was experimenting. I thought she would get over it after the hurt of what Anthony did had worn off." He looked at his wife. "You were worse than I was."

"If Tia's last name had been Trump, Gates, or Buffet, it would have made a difference and you know it. It would have been a lot easier to digest than a former alcohol-abusing, ex-CIA spook who isn't even White Angelo-Saxon Protestant."

Tia began to fume but she decided to hear John's response before she showed herself.

"Doesn't matter. They're giving us an heir. And, honestly, despite all that I felt was initially unacceptable about Tia, she saved Jody's life."

"It wouldn't matter if there wasn't a baby involved. Not with Jody. I don't think it could be more obvious that she is completely head-over-heels in love with Tia. This is the real thing for Jody, and you know it," Sondra said.

"I know it, and now that I've gotten to know Tia, I have to admit that she's a much better 'son-in-law' than Anthony ever was. She's much more committed to Jody—faithful, devoted, protective…" He sighed. "That's all I want for my daughter. My major problem with them was about producing an heir. And now that they've found a way around the procreation issue, I'm thrilled."

"It doesn't bother you that your grandchild will be half brown?"

"Sondra, I don't care if my heir is half Martian. My daughter and her, um, wife…is that what Tia is? Jody's wife?"

"I believe that's the term."

"Why doesn't Jody get to be the wife? She's the smaller and more girly."

"I think they're both wives."

"Oh… well, anyway, they are blissfully happy, and I'm sure that child will want for nothing when it comes to how much the baby will be loved. If it bothers you that your grandchild won't be all white, then you're just going to have to get over it. I'm telling you right now, if you say anything to Jody—"

"Are you going to threaten me with divorce again?"

There was silence and then Tia heard John say, "Just be grateful."

"Are you done blustering?"

"For now."

"Good. Here comes our taxi."

Tia heard the sound of the watercraft nearing *The Quintessence* and no more conversation from her in-laws. She was a little stunned at John's defending her but, clearly, Sondra needed more work. Tia hoped, once the baby was born, Sondra would be past her prejudice. They'd just have to wait and see.

The Aegean Islands

Jody stepped out onto the private balcony off the forward master stateroom. She could have stayed inside the huge bedroom suite and watched the distant village lights from the panoramic, two-hundred-seventy-degree view, but she decided she would rather look at the sky out in the balmy night air. The two-hundred-foot chartered yacht was anchored off Santorini, somewhere between Athinios and Fira in the Cycladic Sea, so the vista was stunning from any perspective, any time of the day or night.

Earlier Jody and Tia had strolled hand-in-hand from the private dining area onto the master deck, which was the location of the pool with its two-level waterfall. They swam naked, savoring the Mediterranean sunset as they enjoyed the warmth of the late spring evening. Sometime between the sun disappearing below the horizon and the full moon rising to illuminate the darkness, they moved to the king-sized berth and made love.

They hadn't been able to go on a honeymoon after the wedding. Montgomery's trial was delayed for months and months by legal motions and continuances. Once it finally began, there were three months of testimony before Montgomery was found guilty of all charges. He was sentenced to over a century of consecutive prison time.

When Jody wasn't testifying or meeting with law enforcement agencies, attorneys, accountants, or publicists, she was busy turning the Montgomery estate into a no-kill pet shelter. She turned the foundation over to Richard and Melanie and helped hire staff and get the facility off the ground.

Life during the months since Jody's rescue had been a whirlwind of passing days, multifarious changes, triumphs, and disappointments. There never seemed to be enough hours in a day for the then-newlyweds to be alone for any extended period of time, which was why they were now as far away from that negative environment as Jody could get, basking in every moment they could spend in each other's presence.

Jody's life had been hectic and complicated, but she knew that everything had worked out the way it was supposed to. She felt a silk robe being placed over her shoulders and snuggled back into the naked form behind her. "It's beautiful here, isn't it?"

"I've never seen anything quite like it."

"Did you want me to come back to bed?" Jody grinned, hopeful.

"Eventually. The air feels good." Tia's arms encircled Jody and caressed her swollen belly. "Besides, our son needs a break."

"Our son will be fine. The doctor said we can have sex right up until I deliver."

"He also said your sex drive would decrease the further along you get."

"No, he said it should decrease, but so far my desire for you hasn't diminished one iota, so…"

A deep, rich laugh sounded just below her ear, followed by kisses tracking along her shoulders. Jody leaned back and tucked her head beneath a strong chin. Hands lovingly massaged the bulging stomach. "He seems to like it when you touch me. He always calms down."

"That's because he knows I'm going to be the disciplinarian in the family. I've seen how your pets have so easily wrapped you around their paws. I can't imagine how you're going to be around our baby. You'll be putty in his tiny little hands."

"Oh, and you won't?"

"Only if he comes out looking exactly like you. Then he might be a little hard to resist."

"Just a little? You're quickly losing points here," Jody said.

"All I'm saying is he might be being born into one of the wealthiest families in the universe, and he might be privileged, but I don't want him growing up and acting as though he's entitled."

"I would never raise him like that." Jody sounded slightly defensive.

"I know you won't. I know we're in full agreement on this. I also know your parents, especially your father, will spoil the sense out of his grandson. You know it, too."

Jody nodded, found a smile, and patted the strong hand that rested on her belly. "Maybe you should be my parents' disciplinarian, too."

"I think it's a little too late for that. Maybe it won't be so bad. They did a pretty good job with you."

"Just pretty good? This honeymoon is getting shorter by the minute," Jody said playfully.

Without relinquishing her embrace, Tia turned Jody until they were face-to-face. She cupped Jody's face and kissed her with all the passion and tenderness a soul could offer. "What can I do to make it up to you, to get things back on track?"

"That's a good start," Jody said breathlessly, as she stood and slowly led Tia back into the bedroom.

Tia's eyes sparkled. "Admit it. You can't quit me."

"You're right, I can't. And I don't want to."

Tia smiled down at her sleeping wife. In two months, Tristan John Ramone Wainwright would be born. John was over the moon at the thought of a grandson, and Sondra appeared to have dropped all her prejudices when she saw the ultrasound photo.

Tia closed her eyes and inhaled the salty fresh air of the Mediterranean Sea. She still couldn't believe how lucky she was.

Hopelessly in love with Jody, Tia found something new every day that made her fall in love with her precious wife a little bit more. Tia was also scared witless of the responsibility and obligation that went with that love. She had told herself she wasn't up to the challenge; she wasn't in Jody's league. She wasn't special enough to hold on to such a gem. She told herself she didn't deserve to have a life this good, she hadn't earned this kind of happiness, when things seemed too good to be true, they usually were. But as she cradled Jody to her while the mother-to-be slept soundly against her breast, Tia felt a rush of pride and euphoria surge through her that always amazed and reassured her. This was exactly where she was meant to be.

Author Cheyne Curry   Photo Credit: Tracy Bricker

About the Author

Cheyne Curry was born in Vermont, raised in New York, and spent most of her adult life in California. She now resides in the Midwest with her partner, Brenda, and their rescued pets Liam (mutt) and Belladonna Bossy Pants (black cat). Cheyne's first novel, *Renegade*, was published in 2009, and was a finalist for the Golden Crown Literary Society Debut Novel Award. Cheyne is also a founding member of 3 Grunts Productions. Their short film, "Survived by…" (written and co-produced by Cheyne) is currently making the rounds of the film festival circuit.

Make sure to check out these other exciting Blue Feather Books titles:

In the Works	Val Brown	978-0-9822858-4-8
Playing for First	Chris Paynter	978-0-9822858-3-1
Two for the Show	Chris Paynter	978-1-9356278-0-7
30 Days Hath September	Jamie Scarratt	978-1-935627-94-4
Appointment with a Smile	Kieran York	978-1-935627-86-9
Possessing Morgan	Erica Lawson	978-0-9822858-2-4
Lesser Prophets	Kelly Sinclair	978-0-9822858-8-6
Come Back to Me	Chris Paynter	978-0-9822858-5-5
A Kiss Before Dawn	Laurie Salzler	978-1-935627-89-0
Confined Spaces	Renee MacKenzie	978-1-9356279-7-5
My Soldier Too	Bev Prescott	978-1-935627-81-4
In the Now	Kelly Sinclair	978-1-935627-85-2
Soulwalker	Erica Lawson	978-1-935627-83-8

www.bluefeatherbooks.com